Black Pages

Black Pages

An Interactive Series of Powerful Short Stories

TINA CRANK-WALTERS

ISBN-13: 978-1502708601
ISBN-10: 1502708604

1. Fiction 2. Relationships

Edited and compiled by Neely Terrell

Printed in the United States of America

This book is dedicated to the readers who are bold enough to live in their own truths of infidelity, addiction, deceit, compromise, and love. It is also for those who would like to.

Author's Note

This body of work hinges on the likeness (with a twist) of individuals whom I have encountered over my lifetime and those whom I have heard stories about. *The Black Pages* will trace topics that transpire in everyday life. If you read closely enough, you just might find your reflection on these black pages.

Contents

My Lover / My Husband (A Bit)

They both hurt me in different ways, yet it felt the same. I lost my sense of direction when I lay with him that day. He dissolved my facade word by word, syllable by syllable, and sound by sound.

I could not breathe in the presence of him and did not want to breathe without him. He was addictive and I had become his addict. He was my necessary hug—my beautiful surprise.

I was positive that it was my newly discovered prowess that controlled my sexual inspiration but soon understood that it was the intrigue of his mind that controlled me instead. It was in that moment when I truly realized that he was the one who temporarily held the power and I became myself no longer.

He was simply exquisite. Until him, no one had ever had the ability to acquire, much less seize, my attention.

Not even my husband.

This man was both my intellectual equal and my mental nemesis. We exchanged soft conversations like easy Sunday mornings. No song and dance, just tender honesty. He was a wealth of information and entertained my unanswered questions with patience. But most importantly, he listened. I was infatuated, but not completely drawn in. He stimulated my thought process and forced me to reckon with the woman that I had become under his deliberate direction.

I used the excuse that my spouse was not a perfect man to escape without guilt, into his core. I later surmised that if the absence of perfection was a consideration for not remaining faithful or married, none of us would be. Nevertheless, with a dominating reckoning, I rediscovered that I was beautiful, powerful, sexy, smart, and physical. Only he was able to pull those influences from the abyss in which I had buried them. I wanted to lose my sanity with him and acknowledged that only he and he alone, could entice me to leave *him*.

As I stroked his wavy hair and softly caressed the strong of his back, I inhaled his scent and photographically etched his face into my mind through my fingertips. I thought, *Only you.*

Feeling the softness of his lips and the sweet acidity of his tongue, I breathed him in as my mind sang. I wanted to permanently take residence inside of his soul and love him from the inside out. When his hardness demanded my wetness, I allowed his thickness inside of me so that we could instantly, yet temporarily, become one.

Once solidified, it was, quite frankly, the rapture. Nothing or no one else had ever compared because he made love to my mind and soul before making love to my body. Therefore, anything physical was secondary. Nervousness had taken control hours before we merged, but the softness of conversation and easiness of mental stimulation long outlasted the penetration, reminding us that a reunion was sure to come.

Then she discovered *we*. You know *her*? Yes, that *she*. She placed him outside his comfort zone which displaced me outside his world. As I struggled to hold on to what was quickly deteriorating, I began to see just how insignificant I was in the whole scheme of his life. She did not want him, but refused to let me have him so, she dangled him before me with a silent reminder of who was truly in control.

Inside of my dreams, I met her.

In our encounter she asked with a quiet assurance, "Are you that *she*?"

As I noted her small facial features and childlike frame, her saddened eyes penetrated my soul and shrank me from the inside out.

"I don't know what I expected, but it was not you," she said. "But I knew that I would find you here."

I could not speak as there was nothing to say. "You have interrupted my life and I need for you to let him go so that he will let go of you."

As the tears kissed her cheeks, my tears did as well. At that moment, I knew that I loved *and wanted* him just as much as she pretended to and letting go would not be that easy.

Dream over.

In reality, she swayed before him his commitment of comfort, kids, and vows. He took the bait and I took a second look at what I had at home: husband, history, drama, tears, and an acceptable unhappiness.

Accepting that life goes on without the lover and could also go on without the husband, I made a choice to live my life without compromise. I chose peace of mind without degradation and the struggle that accompanies being alone. I chose confidence and the faith that I could get the job done unaided.

I chose my own happiness and left my husband to wait for my lover. I knew that after me, it would never be the same with *her* and after he, it would never be the same with *him.* I linger in the moment of us and pray that one day he will tire of being without me as I am of being without him.

Write, share, and discuss with others your thoughts about this bit. What do you think happens next? What emotion surface as you read this short story? Explain why you feel this way.

Raw Addiction (Craig's Story)

Chapter 1

With a mistaken brush of his hand, he unknowingly stimulated my arousal zone. His gesture was simple but my reaction was grand. The lack of panty protection left a wet spot on the back of my silk skirt and in my chair. I was too embarrassed to stand, so I pretended to stay behind to make a phone call while everyone else left the conference room.

Principal Craig was a muscular, six-foot-three illustration of sheer male goodness. He was new to the school and had all the teachers positioning themselves for a piece of what promised to be, if ever granted the opportunity, a first rate lay.

Although he I had to interact throughout the day, after the panty lack incident, I decided that any additional physical contact, if I wanted to remain dry, had to be avoided.

I had never bothered or even felt attracted to another man in my eight years of marriage to Allen, whom I met in college. In my opinion, my life was perfect and aligned with what I had intended for us and our model lives.

"Is anybody sitting here?"

I slowly raised my head from scanning reports to visually receive the mouth that carried such a sultry voice. Although my lips verbalized that the seat was taken, my eyes betrayed them by unabashedly searching his deeply sun-kissed heritage from head-to-toe with a slow and deliberate caress. *It's a damn shame that a man can be that fine and available*, I thought.

I was privy to all the gossip about this beautiful single man, but words alone did not do him justice up close and personal. He was majestic and smelled so good that all I wanted to do was give an on the spot body touch to make sure that he was real.

"Now that you have given me the once-over," he said, interrupting my trail of empty handed caresses. "And you obviously approve. May I now sit?"

"Please do."

"You know," he continued. "It is kind of tough being the new kid on the block around here. Everyone is avoiding me like I have the plague or something." *Yeah, you have the plague alright. A plague that not one woman in this building wouldn't risk catching. They are only staying away because you are a master panty wetter,* thinking to myself. Craig continued.

"Rumor has it that you are the new kid on the block also, so I thought this is as good a time as any to build a relationship with the other newbie."

I cleared my throat. "I am not new on the block. Only new to this position. I have been with the school system for eight years now."

Oh, this guy was beautiful, black, and smooth. I could not focus. I would definitely have to watch myself around him and the best way to do that was to keep my distance. Moving closer, Craig gestured, "Have a bite?" He extended a long french fry towards my mouth while flashing freshly manicured nails.

"No, thanks," I declined. "I like a little more sustenance in my nutrition and only eat from the hands of one man. And he is the man who put this ring on my finger."

Ignoring the latter part of my sentence, he responded, "I can tell that you like to eat healthy because your skin is radiant and your locs are beautifully strong, which seems to be indicative of your personality, as well."

I thought, *You don't know anything about me or my personality,* but opted to remain cordial to one of my many new bosses.

"Forgive my bad manners as I never formally introduced myself. My name is Nelson Craig. I am the sixth grade Assistant Principal. And you are?"

"Nikki Raye. But you already knew that, didn't you?"

He smiled and displayed professionally whitened teeth with a slight gap. For sucking purposes, I decided.

"I have been trying to find an excuse to come over and say hello, Ms. Raye. I noticed you during the presentation and wanted nothing more than to further part your slightly unbuttoned blouse with my finger and slightly caress your beautiful breasts." That's what he was saying in my mind, anyway.

As his lips moved, I continued to create this imaginary conversation in my head. Certain that he could not see it on my cocoa-colored skin, I blushed as my vagina damn cracked and the juices once again started to seep. I was wet and my ladybug was at full attention. I was both speechless and ashamed for feeling so sexual from a fantasy that did not include my husband, but it felt good.

"Ummmm, excuse me, Mrs. Raye. When you find your way back to reality, you might hear your name being paged to the counselor's office."

I was caught off guard and rolled my eyes towards her. The last person that I needed in my space—was that chewing gum popping, school whore, Lisa Dallas. She had talked nonstop about Principal Craig upon his arrival and tagged him gay when he showed no interest in her big booty and thick thighs. She often bragged about how no man could resist her and not too many did. When Craig posed a challenge for her and ignored her advances, he immediately became the foe she wanted to sex only for bragging rights. Excusing himself to leave, Craig greeted Lisa and left my office.

Many of the male teachers had learned the hard way to never trust a big butt and a smile—as New Edition would sing—because if it wasn't good or it was little, Lisa would tell everybody who would listen. *And that was all of us.*

"Thank you Lisa. I really did not hear the page."

"Yeah, I know you didn't," she said, twisting her lips into a smirk. *Okay, here we go,* I thought as she continued. Lisa turned around to show her physique. "Girl, you better leave soft men to the pros like me and get your mind back to Allen before someone else swoop em'up. Think I won't." She winked and mumbled while walking away. Feeling embarrassed and suddenly cheap, I was keenly aware of the silence that had fallen over the teachers' lounge next door to my office and the invisible eyes of its occupants.

The owners of that same piercing silence searched my face for any signs of guilt and surely talked about me as I walked quickly pass the door. I felt like Gloria in *Waiting to Exhale* when she walked away from Gregory Hines back to her house across the street. I'll bet that her drip was as wet as mine then too, but she was probably wearing panties to catch it.

"Glad that you could make it after the tenth intercom page, Nikki," said the head counselor, Gayle Arrington. "I heard that you were dining with the new principal."

"You mean drowning," I corrected, and we both laughed. "Girl, he is fine, right?"

"You better know it." Gayle, a sharp and smart sister who knew her stuff, ran her department with strong yet fair direction. Many coworkers did not always appreciate her candor, but openly respected her as a professional.

Gayle and I became fast friends with the greatest of ease. Our daughters, like we, also became close friends.

"Are we still on for tonight?" Gayle asked. "Allen does not mind me taking up your time for our monthly girl's night out, does he?" I laughed.

"Girl, he looks forward to hanging out alone to watch his soft porn while I am gone. Just as much as I enjoy reaping the benefits when I return. It is a win-win situation for everyone involved." We both laughed.

"The reason that I paged was to let you know that you have been selected to attend the Counselors Conference in New Orleans in a couple of weeks. It is a five-day conference, so make sure to give Allen all of the love and affection that he can handle so that your arch enemy, Lisa, won't be trying to back-door your ass. Because girl you know that she has her eyes on your man and Principal Craig. I am just waiting for her to tell me that at least one of them gave bad sex so that I won't feel so bad for never being able to get some from either one of them," she joked. *I think that was a joke.*

"Well, I can assure you Gayle, that she will not deliver any news to you about Allen because I know what my man is holding and who he is holding it for. You can believe a sister on that," I nodded.

"Well go head then. I ain't mad at ya."

"Now, getting back to the matter at hand, I am not sure who will attend the conference with you. The rumor mill is that Stanley Jeffers will be attending with you because I will already be in D.C."

"No, Gayle!" I said, not trying to hide my disappointment.

"Nikki, I tried my best to get that trip changed so that we could party all night in the Big Easy and then go to the conference still drunk as mofo's, but I was turned down flat. Just make sure that you party enough for the both of us and watch out for the Creole men," Gayle joked. "I heard they love chocolate sisters with the tight booties and long legs."

"Doesn't everybody?" I joked back and started to walk out of the door.

"Hey," Gayle called out. "Would you mind dropping this package at Mr. Jeffers' office on your way back?"

"No problem," I said and walked away, promising to meet her that night.

While walking back, I caught a reflection of my slim stature in the glass window. My physique had changed since college, but I still kept my long and lean swimmer's body that helped me to win a four-year athletic scholarship. I had always prayed for a shapelier backside, but nature envisioned a need to put it in front with a size 36DD breast that was accentuated by a 24" waist. Allen loved the way my breasts looked in- and out of my clothes and never missed an opportunity to bury his face or his manhood in between my two mounds of soft flesh.

Straightening my clothes, I noticed that my nipples were erect from thinking about Allen sucking and playing with them, so I decided to take a detour to my office and call my husband for a little phone sex.

Feeling satisfied shortly thereafter, I kissed Allen through the phone, sucked the juices from my fingers and proceeded to drop off the package.

As I moved closer to Stanley's office, I heard lowered voices, one which sounded like Principal Craig. "We will discuss this after school hours, as your actions were inappropriate and borderline unprofessional, Stanley."

I wanted them to go on, but Lisa called me out from down the hall, which abruptly ceased all conversation and made the attention immediately turn to me. Damn.

"Nikki, may I help you?" Principal Craig asked. Forgetting for a moment why I was standing there, I once again took in his extreme beauty and striking features and was immediately mesmerized.

"Girl, snap out of it!" Lisa yelled. "Answer the man and stop jockeying!" Giving her a go-to-hell look and her giving it back, I passed the package to Craig.

"Counselor Arrington asked me to give this to Mr. Jeffers. I apologize for the interruption."

Walking away, I could not help but think that I had interrupted something that was very juicy and important. I made a mental note to find out just who was this thin, white, and slightly balding man and what he had said to offend Principal Craig to cause him to assert his alpha male authority, which excited me. I went home to give my husband the benefits of that excitement, which another man had stirred up inside of me.

Enjoying a marathon evening of passionate lovemaking, Allen and I finally came up for air and escaped to the kitchen for a quick bite of freshly sliced peaches, melon, and a glass of wine. We eased into conversation about our day at work and completing the colorful décor of our newly purchased home. With most rooms empty except for two of the six bedrooms and kitchen, our huge house was the perfect nesting ground for christening. We had just finished room number five and had at least five more to go.

"I am so glad that we married, Nikki. You know, most couples don't get the opportunity to marry their true love, like we did. We held on through college and now have the perfect life. You are so beautiful and funny. I don't ever want to be with another woman, because you are all the woman that I need." Touching me lovingly, he asks, "Am I all the man that you need?"

My innocent husband was playing with a slow burn and did not realize that he was setting the scene for a smiling lie. I did a quick once-over and felt myself melt for his sweet ignorance. After all, I am the best sex that he has ever had. Why wouldn't he need only me? It was my job to make him think that. And I was damn good at it. Getting pointers from my older and more seasoned friends, I often tried out their sexual escapades on him and received accolades.

"Yes, Allen, you are all the man that I need." Channeling my Whitney Houston archives, I continued. "You fill me up and have given me more love than I've ever imagined. You are truly all the man that I need." And he was, *until I locked eyes with Craig*. "Allen?" Moving in closer, I lay my head on his chest. "May I ask you question?"

"Anything", he replied.

"Do you trust me?"

"Yes, with every inch of my being."

"Then close your eyes", I said. He obediently obliged. As I pulled the silk scarf from my locs to cover his eyes, I fed him my ladybug topped whipped cream. He licked it up like a pro. As my body shuttered and released inside his mouth, I instantly wondered if Craig would like the flavor of my love juice as much as Allen does.

Awakened by a banging on the door, Allen and I slowly moved from our slumber on the kitchen floor to cover our nakedness. As I peeped out the keyhole, I saw the middle finger of Gayle.

"Oh shit," I winced.

"Who is it?" Allen asked.

"It's Gayle."

"I stood her up tonight," I whispered.

"Yeah, bitch, open the door. I hear you in there!"

As I slowly opened the door, Gayle only had to take one quick look around at the empty whipped cream can, old fruit, and empty wine bottles to know why I did not show. Her mouth was full of trash talk, but her eyes said that I understand.

"Aww, hell, Nikki. I ain't even mad no more." We laughed and embraced with a quick hello. "Girl, you smell like old sex and alcohol. I just picked up Kerie from the sitter's and thought that I'd stop by to cuss you out for not answering your phone or calling to say you wouldn't make it."

"Gayle, I am so sorry. The night flew by so swiftly and I just forgot that we had plans. Allen made it so easy to stay home tonight. I honestly forgot." She rolled her eyes to dismiss me and I felt a little tug on my robe. I looked down to see Gayle's daughter Kerie.

"Hi Kerie. How are you? You look so pretty."

"Thanks," she said. "Where is Alena?"

"She is sleeping, but I'll bet if you run upstairs to her room, she'll wake up for you."

"Gayle, she is growing so fast and leaving my little Alena behind. It seems as if they were just born yesterday and it has been four years now for my Alena and your Kerie. I am so happy we are friends. I feel as if I have known you all of my life. Sit down and I will fix you some late night breakfast."

"I'll fix the night breakfast," Gayle said. "You go shower and get the funk off your ass, you dirty bird. Plus, I saw Allen slip out quietly through the back stairs. He's probably gone back to sleep, so this is a perfect time for us to discuss your trip to New Orleans and my trip to D.C." Gayle rolled her eyes. "Nikki, wouldn't it be fun if we could make that trip to New Orleans together?"

"*Shhh*!" I said, pulling Gayle away from the base of the stairs as if Allen was listening.

"What do you mean, '*shhh*'?"

"I have not mentioned the trip to Allen yet and I don't want to tell him today. Maybe tomorrow."

"Nikki, what are you waiting for? I am confused. Don't you think that the more advanced notice, the better?"

"I guess, Gayle. It's just that he gets so whiney and needy when I have to leave on business trips and the later I tell him, the less that I have to hear about it."

"I hear that. See, it's times like these when I am happy to be single because I don't have to answer to no man about taking care of business. Just my Momma," she said jokingly.

"Seriously," she continued. "I would be lost without Momma. She has been here for me and Kerie. Kerie's

Dad and I were not together when he passed of AIDS. I thank God every day that we managed to escape the contraction. You know, I had been married for ten years before divorcing without children. Then along came a one-night-freak-session-of-divorced celebration, which brought about my pregnancy and joy. My joy turned to sadness when it was rumored that her Dad had the virus and was not telling his lovers of his illness. I became more distraught when I realized it was true".

Drifting into a state of reminisce. "I thought I was going to die, Nikki. It was the absolute worse time of my life. But God is good and He is faithful to those who are faithful to Him. So, between God and Momma's prayers to Him, both Kerie and I escaped with our health intact. Although it has been almost five years now, Kerie and I still get tested every six months just for peace of mind. He confessed to full blown AIDS two years ago died shortly thereafter. I have not had a relationship since and I really don't want one. I am happy with my vibrator until I can get past the dishonesty and betrayal. Chile' no man deserves my baggage. But enough about me, go shower and get dressed so that we can talk the rest of the night away about happy things!"

Standing in the shower and processing what Gayle had just told me, it suddenly occurred to me how deadly the ramifications of infidelity, unprotected sex, and promiscuity can be to the trusting and unsuspecting. I also realized that I really do not know what secrets Craig might have. Yet, my mind kept roaming back to him. I was already drawn to his scent, captivated by his smile, and loved the way his body moved underneath his custom fitted pants. I had a raw addiction and was perplexed as to how the mere thought of him could instantly wet my inner thighs so soon after a passionate episode of lovemaking with my husband. Thinking of Craig, I quietly masturbated in the shower, kissed my husband goodnight as he slept, and hurried back downstairs.

With late night turning into early morning, Gayle decided to sleep over for some early shopping the next day. After a long day of fun and food with Gayle and the girls, I was happy to get home and relax. Allen, waiting like a good husband, had prepared dinner and was eagerly awaiting our return. After a nice meal and putting Alena to bed, he passed a letter to me.

"What is this?" I asked.

"A Principal Craig stopped by today."

My heart skipped and sweat lightly covered my brow as I stopped breathing for a split second.

"He dropped off your itinerary for the New Orleans Conference next week." His slightly elevated voice suggested more it was more of a question than a statement. "I was surprised to hear about it. Especially, since you are leaving next Monday. Is there something that you would like to share, Nikki?" I sat silently as he clinched his teeth. "He said that the date had been moved up and you would need to leave Sunday morning." Reaching out to touch his hands, Allen pulled away.

"Why did he have to come to our home for that, Allen?" I attempted to sound annoyed to mask the disappointment that I felt for not being here to see him. "They're making house calls now?"

"That's not what is important. When were you going to tell me about this, Nikki? I am your husband, right? I do deserve to know what is going on with you, don't I?"

"Allen." I made another attempt to reach his hands. "I am sorry for not telling you right away, but you always get upset and make me feel guilty for leaving. I just thought that if I did not tell you right away, I would not have to hear the complaints about my leaving. I just wanted to enjoy you as much as possible this week without any conflict or pressure. Please baby, don't be angry. Especially since I have to leave sooner than planned."

Even though I was certain that he wanted to, Allen never spoke another word about my trip for the rest of the week and it was a nice change of pace. I awakened late the morning of my flight and was in a rush to get to the airport on time. I decided to pack smart and light the night before with only black slacks, a black skirt, black pumps, and blazer for the cool rooms. It all fit into one bag and I was ready to roll. Instead of rushing to get everyone up and out the house, I called a cab and kissed my family goodbye with promises to call as soon as we touched down.

I thanked God for the light Atlanta traffic at 6:00am on a Sunday morning and cussed the idiot who changed the itinerary from Monday evening to Sunday morning.

Once at the airport, I made the mad dash from check-in to the concourse train, only to find that the flight was delayed for another 45 minutes. Thankful for the delay, I walked over to Starbucks for a mint mocha chip frappucino and slice of lemon cake to help bring calmness to my rushed spirit.

It was a refreshing change to watch others run through the airport trying to catch their flights before the entry doors closed.

"Nice locs," I heard someone say.

Silently cussing the stranger that had invaded my calmness, I looked up to see a bow-tie wearing, rimmed-glasses-sporting, six-foot-two or taller, Nation of Islam follower.

"Thanks," I said, and looked away. He was unmoved and decided to continue.

"Why are you drinking a cup of liquid that the white man told us we needed in order to prove assimilation to white society?"

"Negro, what?" I questioned. "You sound like an idiot".

I repositioned myself where my back completely faced him and took another sip. He interrupted again. "Sister, why do you want to perpetuate the wastefulness that has tricked African Americans into believing they need to pay four dollars for the white man's interpretation of societal acceptance?"

Looking around to see if this character was serious and if I was being punked, I noticed that he had created a captive audience of mostly white onlookers. Not willing to endure the energy that it would take to engage this anxious man in conversation, I called for airport security. He was escorted away and I continued to enjoy my perpetuated wastefulness to the fullest.

Drinking my last sip of warmth, the announcement came that Flight 247 from Atlanta to New Orleans was boarding. I rushed to the restroom, did my business, washed my hands, and boarded the plane. As I made my way to coach, I wondered if Mr. Jeffers would be arriving soon. I was so caught up in Nation of Islam dude that I did not think to look around to see if my flight mate was watching like everyone else. As the people begin to settle, I wondered if Mr. Jesser, like I, had slept late and possibly missed the flight. I could only hope. As I placed my headphones over my ears and lay back to relax away my flight anxieties, a light tap on my shoulder forced me to open my eyes. It was Gayle. I could not contain myself and jumped to hug her before she sat down.

"How in the hell?"

"Don't ask," she said. "Just know that it is on like popcorn!"

"New Orleans here we come!"

We slept the entire flight and awakened with a new energy of excitement. We checked into our connecting hotel rooms, changed into our sexy clothes, and went to walk the strip at 10:00am. Once we realized that Bourbon Street was still sleeping, we changed into our comfortable shoes and headed towards the pier. On our way, we found a twenty-four hour blues bar where we drank, smoke, and ate the best damn gumbo ever. Full of energy, we walked the pier, met strangers, and flirted. After wearing ourselves out in a record two hours, we made our way back to the hotel and crashed into our rooms until dusk.

"It's time to go, girl," Gayle said, opening the adjoining door. "The night is just getting started! Get your lazy ass up and let's roll."

"Gayle, you never said how was it that you got here."

"Nikki, remember when I stopped by, I knew then and was planning to surprise you with the news until you revealed that you had not mentioned it to Allen. I was not sure if he was going to convince you that you needed to stay home and I did not want to be part of the argument, even without being there. So, I decided not to tell you."

"Gayle, I am so surprised and happy you came. I just knew that Stanley would show and was not looking forward to it."

"Nikki, do you like these earrings?" Gayle asked, changing the subject. "I bought them at a gift shop in the airport while I was ducking and hiding from you. What was up with Bow-Tie?"

"I don't know, Gayle."

"I thought I was going to have to come out of hiding to do a *con-fu* on his ass." As she proceeded to demonstrate with a mid-air karate chop, we both laughed ourselves into tears then left the room to join the nightlife of New Orleans.

"I am not sure what happened with Stanley Jeffers, but Dr. Newman told me that I was going in his place without explanation and that Principal Craig, with his fine panty-wetting ass, was going to D.C."

"I don't wet my panties for him", I winked.

"Oh girl, please. Everyone knows that this man is quietly feeling you and if you were not married, you would have done the dirty deed with him a long time ago. Lisa thinks that you already have, but we know what you got at home, don't we?"

I smiled, but did not protest much because Gayle was right. He did make my panties wet and if I had to chance to see *it*, I would probably look.

Not being in New Orleans since the early nineties brought back a strong sense of freedom. I felt like a college student kicking it with my best girl who was down for whatever. It was going to be a fun ride with Gayle. We must have dipped in and out of at least twelve establishments before settling on this little Blues Café on Bourbon Street. The café was dark and smoky with some of the best live blues I'd ever heard. After our fill of crawfish and crabs, Gayle and I settled into what seemed like endless rounds of appletini's and vodka and cranberry.

"Gayle, I am so glad that you are here with me," I slurred. "I cannot think of anyone else that I would like to get out of control with. We are going to have to bring a recorder to the conference in the morning just to make sure that we get the information."

Gayle agreed, while expressing her interests for getting laid. She had caught the eyes of a silk-shirt-wearing, dirty-shoe-sporting, home-grown Creole. And the way that she was smiling at him, made it almost look as if he had a chance. I interrupted their eye contact by waving my hand in front of her face.

"Gayle, you cannot be seriously thinking about going there."

"Why not?" She asked. "I just want to have fun and frankly, comfort as many penises as I can in one week. I got my supply of condoms and my mace, if they get out of control. But on the real, I just want to release some tension on a man—and not a dildo—for a change." After all she'd been through, she deserved it. So, I chose not to remind that it was just last week that she expressed being content with her man-less life.

Gayle had always portrayed herself as such a strong and independent image that it never occurred to me that she might want or need the touch of a man every once in a while. As I searched her face, her eyes pleaded with me not to intervene. Clearly thinking that the broken eye contact would ruin whatever chance he might have for free sex, he began to walk over. I listened long enough to hear that he truly was the loser up-close that he portrayed far away said nothing when he asked Gayle to dance. As I watched them walk away, I noticed how when placed in a true social setting, Gayle, like any other woman, searched for validation and affection, no matter how unattractive the source.

"You look as if you so deep in thought that I'm almost afraid to approach you." I turned to see a fair-skinned, heavy set woman smiling at me. It was obvious from her heavily influenced accent that she was home grown. "I thought that she was your girl until I saw Sneed take her to the floor."

"Sneed?" I asked.

"That's right. Can I sit?"

"Not sure." I said without interest.

With obviously a preference for women, she embraced male clothing, including a wallet in the back pocket, but wore the very sensuous Amarige fragrance. Her hair was cut low to the scalp. She was pretty, in a masculine kind of way, with braces and breasts.

"You like Wynton and Aaron? Or are you more of a BB kind of woman?"

Never being approached by a woman before, I was too curious to not allow her to sit, but not curious enough to engage her in any bullshit conversation.

"What do you want?" I asked.

"I want to get to know you. Where are you from and what's your name?"

I motioned for her to sit down. "That's what I'm talking bout'. It's about time you showed a sista-bro some love." She repositioned herself. "My name is Arieal Tibadeau. My grandaddy owns this joint and I know just about ere'body who walks through these doors, if dey' from her'. When I saw you my shit starting jumping off like I was at the strip club watchin' bitches pole and I knew that I had to get on through her' to say sum'n. So, what's the deal, is you down or what?"

Watching Gayle and this manly woman facing me, I responded that I was not into licking women. I get licked.

"It ain't no thang. Shit, it would do me proud jus' to smell on your fine ass." Out of nowhere came a fist to the face of Arieal that knocked her to the floor and forced me to stand.

"Bitch, how you gon' say it's over in one minute and try to trick this bitch the next?" Getting up from the floor with the bouncer trying to make his way through the gathering crowd, I slowly backed away not wanting to miss the action but knowing that I needed to find Gayle.

I looked for Gayle, pushing my way through the crowd as Arieal punched her ex-girlfriend to the floor, jumped on top, and began pounding her in the face. In the midst of the shuffling, I caught a glimpse of who could have been Stanley Jeffers. When I finally caught up with Gayle outside, she was in an awkward protection-like embrace with Sneed.

"Nikki!" Gayle waved me over. "This is Sneed."

"I know. Arieal told me all about him before she decided to give her ex-girl the beat down."

Sneed avoided eye contact and dropped his head. Staring at Gayle, I almost anticipated her next request.

"Girl, would you mind if Sneed and I went off for some drinks since this party is obviously over?" I gave her the *"Are you serious?"* look and pulled her out of his arms and to the side for a quick chat.

"Gayle, not him!" I begged. "According to Arieal, he is the local club rat who has absolutely nothing going for himself. Arieal said that he is always in the club pimping unsuspecting women just like you. Let's keep moving, Gayle. This guy is a zero." Of course none of this was not true, but I was trying to build my case against Steed.

"Everybody can't be like you, Nikki. Sneed makes me feel attractive and he makes me laugh. I am not trying to be his girl. I just want to have a good time, NikNik." She played the term of endearment card. "Plus, I felt his stuff and he has a big one."

"Yes. A big one laced with what STD?" Not offended as she should have been with my smart remark. "Girl, stop trippin'. We are going back to the room after we get our drinks, so make sure you close the adjoining door."

Not winning this argument, I asked Sneed for his cell phone number, which I called while he was standing there, and to see his ID, where I took down his address, just in case Gayle did not show up the next day.

Bidding Gayle good bye for the evening and calling her a traitor in the same breath, I slowly began to walk back to the room while taking in the ambience of the city. It was breathtakingly beautiful, full of culture and fun. By the time I made it back to the room, it was 2:00am.

I showered and decided to call Allen and Alena in the morning before leaving for the conference. I was exhausted, but glad to be out of town away from Craig as he was never too far away from my thoughts. Before I lay my hot body onto that cold and empty bed, I remembered Gayle's toys and went into her room to borrow one of her many toys that she joked were her male prostitutes.

Searching through her items, I was surprised to see so many different shapes and sizes of vibrators and opted to select the soft fleshy one with the tickler.

Showering, I washed Gayle's juices away and replaced them with my own. The running water from the hot and steamy shower masked my moans. Walking back to replace the vibrator, I switched on some jazz and stopped just short of opening the door when I overheard Gayle's and Sneed's impatient moans of passion escape through the door cracks and the walls.

Attempting to peek, by quietly cracking the adjoining door, I was disappointed to find it locked. I sat quietly on the floor and listened as the sounds of their skin on skin elevated the actual act. Beginning to feel the wetness between my own thighs once again, I lay on the floor in the darkness, spread my legs, pressed the vibrator against myself and received their moans until my own sounds began to softly escape from my lips. Matching their rhythmic moans, my body tensed and exploded while Gayle's muffled screams indicated that she too had begun to explode. Then Sneed followed suit. The three of us shared raw sex that night, but only one of us would ever know.

6:45am came too early for two women who had drank and sexed themselves into a stupor, but we managed to get dressed, grab coffee from downstairs and head across the street to the conference.

"How did you sleep last night?" Gayle asked.

"Not very well, since I heard every bump and grind that you and Mr. McDirty shared last night."

Gayle seemed embarrassed.

"Oh please, Gayle. Don't get embarrassed now. I am sure that you were not thinking about me when he had his head all up in your nappy dugout. And I hope that you did not reciprocate. Did you even look at it before you let him? You did use a condom, right?"

Gayle seemed annoyed. "Damn girl, can I get in a response or what? How do you know where he had his head last night and what business of it is of yours if I had mine there?"

"Gayle, as long as it has been for you, I am sure the nappy dugout was the first line of business."

"You know that's right," she said while giving me a high five. "Listen, Nikki, he might not be the finest mug, but he knows how to work that tongue and that body. He laid pipe like he was replacing the plumbing. I cannot make apologies for having a good time. His sex was the *shiiiiiit!* And I'm going to get some more while I'm here. I have not been turned out like that in years and have not had an orgasm with a man since my baby-daddy. So you can say what you want and hear what you want, but I am playing catch up and cannot wait to see him tonight and every night until I am back in Atlanta. So, get over it and let's you and me chill in the early hours and him and me in the wee hours, okay?"

"Gone girl, do your thang", I said while feeling a little envious. "Do your thang."

Sitting and listening to the facilitator, Gayle and I used a recorder for most of our note taking and wrote only when we knew that we needed elaboration on a specific topic. Before they announced our next speaker, Gayle and I took a quick bathroom break and overheard two women talking about the fine ass man in the hallway and hoped that he was the next speaker so that they could get a better look at him.

"His ass is as tight as a rubber band and he is for real sporting that bald head", I heard one of them say. Leaving the bathroom, Gayle and I were silently communicating that we wanted to get a glimpse just in case he was not the speaker and hurried out the door, bumping each other on the way. To our dismay, he was gone by the time we made it to the hallway, so we took our seats.

When Principal Craig walked onto the stage, Gayle and I could not believe what or who we were seeing and happily stood when he acknowledged us as part of his team. As I turned around, I caught the eyes and two thumbs up from the women who were in the restroom. I smiled as if I had immediately, without words, staked my claim.

"Nikki, sit your obvious ass down," Gayle said. "You are waving like you just won a pageant or something. He is not your man."

"Gayle, did you know that he was coming?"

"Girl, now you know that I would have told you if I had known that Craig was coming. He was supposed to take my place with Jeffers, in D.C. this week. Maybe he came here for you, Nikki."

Pretending not to hear her, I changed the subject. "Speaking of Jeffers, I said, I could have sworn that I saw him at the Café last night when the fight broke out."

"What, Nikki? Girl, that was those appletini's talking to you last night or a Jeffers look-a-like. You know we all have one. I am sure that he is sitting in a conference room checking out some man's ass."

"Gayle, what are you talking about?"

"Girl, rumor has it that he is gay, but you did not hear me say it."

"Whatever, Gayle. Each to his or her own," I replied.

I had other things on my mind and it had nothing to do with the conference. While still trying to get over the fact that Craig had pulled a quick one on us and managed to keep it quiet, I could not help but think how nice it would be to spend time with him in New Orleans for a few days away from prying eyes. My wishes were put to rest when Craig thanked the audience for their attentiveness and stated that he had to catch a plane back to Atlanta in a few hours.

Closing out the first day of the conference on a positive note, Gayle and I, like many other women, made a beeline to greet Craig. The two ladies managed to out run everyone and engaged Craig in conversation first. After realizing that he was single, they tried to convince him to remain in New Orleans for one night on the town or at least for a drink before his flight. He politely declined and began to move towards Gayle's and my direction but was stopped by another principal.

Anxious to get dinner and drinks with me over and back to Sneed, Gayle encouraged me to wave a quick hello to Craig while pulling me out of the door.

"Can you believe that he is here, Gayle?"

"No, can you?" She asked sarcastically.

"What is that supposed to mean?"

"You know. You cannot tell me that you do not wish that he was staying. I bet your panties begin to moist when you saw him."

I remained silent as Gayle, whom I had known far less than most of my long term friends, somehow knew me best where Craig was concerned and the effect that he had on me.

"Well, before you entertain going there with him, Nikki, just remember that you have someone just as fine at home who loves and cherishes the ground that you walk on and any woman, outside of you it seems, would be glad to have him. Just remember that."

"Actually, I am glad that Craig is going back to Atlanta tonight simply for that reason".

Dinner and drinks moved quickly with Gayle and like clockwork, Sneed showed up to swoop her way. This time, he was taking her to see the sites of New Orleans before the sexcapades. Once again, I asked to see his ID to make sure that it did not change and asked to see his proof of his auto insurance. I was not sure why. It just seemed like the right thing to do. He seemed somewhat annoyed but I reminded him that my only concern was for my friend Gayle and nothing more. Gayle, who was obviously touched, hugged my neck and thanked me for being such a good friend. Since we would be leaving New Orleans in a few of days, Gayle promised that we would go shopping tomorrow after the conference and whispered that she would try to be really quiet when then returned later.

Walking back to the hotel, the air felt a little breezy and cool. I called Allen and Alena and shared my day with them and the sights of the city. I sent pictures of interesting sites through my camera phone with little messages. The conversation was light and easy and he asked me if I had been watching the news.

"Apparently, there is a storm brewing, that is showing signs of a potential hurricane," he said. "So, make sure that you pay close attention to the news as they say that it could possibly become a hurricane within a week or less."

I promised Allen that I would monitor the news and at the first sign of trouble, get on the first flight to Atlanta. The familiarity and concern of his voice made me miss him and reflect on the conversation that Gayle and I had earlier about my caring husband. I began to long for his touch. He promised to call me back after putting Alena to bed for some phone sex. I was happy with that and began to count down the hours.

"How are you enjoying the city, Mrs. Raye?" Asked the friendly hotel clerk with the gold teeth and gelled updo.

"Such a beautiful place," I responded. "It has been years since I visited here. Have you heard any more news about this tropical storm, Katrina?"

"Yes," she eagerly said. "The newsman said that it will probably turn away from us in tha' next 24 hours. So, I ain't really worried no more. You know we have had so many close calls, before that, so no one really takes it seriously. I live wit' my Grandma, and she was telling me about a big hurricane in here and how the water came and she lost everything that she had, but stayed because New Orleans is all that she know. She said she gon' die here. I guess I kind of feel tha' same way. I love it here and don't have no real plans to leave," she went on. "My grandma raised me when my Momma ran out and left me and now I got my own baby. So, I guess it's just meant for us to keep our line in New Orleans."

I could not help but to wonder exactly how much of this beautiful city did she actually get to see and appreciate when she was not working. And if a hurricane really did come, would she indeed remain for the sake of her irrational grandmother, while putting both herself and her child's life in jeopardy? I bid her a good evening and wished her well. As I headed for the elevator, the clerk called my name.

"Mrs. Raye," she called. As I stopped and turned around, she was holding flowers. "These for you. A man came by here lookin' for you and tha' other lady saying that he was not sure if y'all were at this hotel. He left a note and these flowers for you and said to tell you congratulations."

"Congratulations? What did he look like, please?"

"Oh my goodness!" Fanning herself as to cool off, she began to describe him. "He was tall and dark-black-skinned with a bald head. He was a fine hot chocolit'. Oh, so fine. He looked like he stepped out of tha'magazine. That's him right there!"

Turning towards the door, I came face-to-face with the one man who could make me cheat on my husband with no regrets.

"Craig?" My body felt hot. "How are you?" I wanted to hug him but remained acutely aware that we were under scrutiny. As we shook hands, my eyes made him aware that were being watched also. We hugged professionally and I thanked him openly for the fake congratulatory flowers.

"Craig, I thought that you were on your way back to Atlanta, I whispered. Why are you still here?"

"Well, before I saw you this afternoon, I had every intention of flying back to Atlanta, but as the flight time grew closer, I could not seem to leave the city without first seeing if I could well, frankly, spend some one on one time with you.

"You do know that I'm married?"

"If I have crossed the line by asking, Nikki, please say so and I will leave. I really do not want to risk losing our blossoming friendship before it has been fully defined." *Fully defined, I thought. What an interesting choice of words.*

"Can we go somewhere?" He whispered. I reminded him that I could not allow him to escort me to my room under the circumstances.

I quietly asked him to meet me around the side entrance of the building so that we could take the stairs to my room. We openly said good night and he left for the side door. As I turned to walk away, the clerk said, "I don't know bout' you, but I woulda took him upstairs, husband or not."

I feel the exact same way, I thought. *But there is no need to share that with you.* Both excited and nervous, I was happy to be away from the sights of the desk clerk and was now relieved that Gayle was away with Sneed. I did not want to have to answer to anyone for what I was obviously about to do and her not being here made it easier to believe that it was alright. Only God himself would have to intervene to make me stop and it seemed that He was not ready to teach me a lesson just yet.

After letting Craig inside, he hugged me softly at the side doorway and grabbed my hand as we walked up the stairs in silence. I walked faster than I normally would as I did not want anyone to witness me with Craig other than on a professional level. Mostly all participants were staying at the same hotel, including the two women whom we overheard in the ladies restroom during the conference. *Dirt is best hidden under a rug and this was exactly where I was going to sweep mine and leave it,* I thought,

Once we made it safely to the room, I locked the door to the adjoining room and motioned for Craig to make himself comfortable while I showered. As the water flowed over my sweltering body, my mind began to research and fast forward all of the reasons why I should not have this man in my room, but my body would not listen and overruled my mind. Pulling back the shower curtain, I checked my slender body, for wet spots and towel dried my long locs. Craig had located my fragrance sticks. The scent of patchouli filled the room and seeped underneath the bathroom door. I lotion by body down with earth scents, clipped my pubic hair and brushed my teeth. I felt like a teenager who was about to get my first piece.

The phone rang. It was Allen calling for our phone sex date. I motioned for Craig to not make a sound, as I tried to think of a reason that I could not have phone sex with my husband. When I could not, I decided to go with the flow. As I watched Craig watch me, his expression of interest changed to excitement when he saw me preparing to have phone sex with my husband.

"What you are doing now?" Allen asked in his sultry voice.

"I am lighting the candles and turning out the lights, baby. Yes, the patchouli is already burning. Ooh yes, Allen, I want you too."

"What are you doing now, Nikki?"

"I am disrobing and walking towards the bed, Allen." As I walked past Craig, he slapped my ass. Passion had embraced him and lust had taken full control of his manhood. I unbuttoned Craig's pants as Allen told me that he was unbuttoning his.

"Grab your penis for me, baby." Allen and Craig both obliged. "Now stroke it up and down. Does it feel good, Daddy?" They both said yes and I continued. "Now imagine my tongue moving slowly up and down your shaft, Allen. Can you feel it?"

Allen said yes. Craig's head went back as my tongue slowly moved up and down his shaft. "Now grab a hold and move it up and down, ok, Daddy?" They both said ok.

"Allen, I am now on the bed with my legs open wide. I am so wet that your mouth could probably bathe in it. Talk to me, Daddy." I clicked on the speaker as Allen began.

"Do you feel my tongue on your breast, softly nibbling and tugging on your nipples?"

"Yes, I feel it."

Craig followed Allen's direction and began to nibble and suck my breast. I moaned.

"I am now moving my tongue down your stomach while kissing you lightly on your sides."

"And I am moving my feet rapidly up and down your shaft. Do you feel that, Daddy?" My voice deepened. He moans and I knew that he was close. "Hold on, Daddy. We must come together, ok?" He moans a throaty moan as we proceed.

"Nikki," Allen said. "Your wetness smells so good. I just want to stick my tongue in it."

"Then do it, baby," I directed. Craig does in reality what Allen does in imagination. I melt and begin to thrust myself against the pulses of Craig's tongue and Allen's words. We lose speech and get lost in each other's lust. Allen, Craig, and I share one incredible orgasm that was released to the universe-our desires blending into one sound.

Allen and I said goodnight. I promised to call him tomorrow.

Craig moved in quickly and entered into me with the aggression of a sexual predator. His manhood is long and thick. I was consumed and matched his thrusts with overzealous enthusiasm. I wanted to be completely filled with him. I did not want to stop. We moved like animals throughout the room as if there was no tomorrow. He entered every orifice without losing rhythm. When we orgasm occurred again, we lost our souls to one another. I could no longer tell where his semen began and where my juices ended. We were the liquid that sealed the broken half of two hearts and now harbored one body and one soul. We never spoke during the entire act as there simply were no words.

Lying in darkness, I decided to mention to Craig that I thought I saw Jeffers at the blues Café'. He jokingly responded that although everyone loves New Orleans, he doubted that Jeffers would be here. His lack of concern was contagious and we never spoke of it again. After he dressed, we embraced and held one another longer than the average one night stand because we knew there would be more. When he left, I locked the door and lay naked on my bed pressing the rewind button in my mind's eye, promising myself that we would have to use a condom next time. I had shared sex twice in one week with now four people who were not aware that I was listening nor cheating. Both times I felt dirty, yet satisfied.

On our way to the conference the next morning, I didn't know who looked worse, Gayle or me. We both said very little to one another until after the third cup of coffee. We had been monitoring the tropical storm Katrina which had now been upgraded to hurricane status. The conference concluded early and we prepared to leave on the earliest flight the next morning to avoid being stranded.

Gayle and I canceled shopping and watched the residents of New Orleans as they were busily preparing for the storm, boarding up their businesses and homes.

The city was abuzz and Mayor Ray Nagin was on the news instructing the citizens of New Orleans not to panic. The city was under mandatory evacuation. He encouraged everyone who could, to leave the city within the next 48 hours and discussed alternate plans for the residents who could not evacuate.

"What do think is going to happen with all of this stuff going on, Gayle? What will happen to the people here if the city floods? Is Sneed staying or leaving?"

Ignoring my first two questions, Gayle informed me that she had asked Sneed to join her in Atlanta. I was both speechless and appalled.

"After two days of sex, do you think you are in love? Are you crazy? What do you know about this guy? You have not even checked his credit and you are trying to set him up at your place? Girl, you are tripping over some you-know-what! Are you going to bring this dude around your little girl? Can you trust him not to put his hands on her? Have you thought about that, Gayle?"

Gayle coldly and quickly responded, "Were you thinking about your little girl or Allen when you were having sex with Craig last night, Nikki?"

Caught off guard, I froze for a split second.

"I know why you look like shit today, Nikki. I saw Craig leaving the hotel early this morning when Sneed dropped me off. What? You weren't going to tell me? How are you going to rag me about sleeping with Sneed when you gave it up to your boss? What about your husband?"

Feeling indignant, humiliated, and trapped, I responded that her sex was probably the sex of pity and that Sneed saw her as an opportunity because he knew that she could not do any better. And once he had taken all of her money and used her up, he would leave her for a better and younger Atlanta bitch. I regretted it immediately, but could not take it back. She said that she felt sorry for me and walked away, leaving me sitting alone and feeling dirty, caught, and stupid.

By the time I made it back to the room, Allen had left messages on both the cell phone and the hotel phone begging me to take the next flight out. When I called, he answered on the first ring.

"Hello?"

"Hey, honey. Nikki," Allen sounded panicked. "Where were you?"

"I was out with Gayle, Allen. I am trying to get on the next flight out, but all the airlines numbers are either busy or have a long wait time. I am almost finished packing and am heading to the airport to see if I can get on the next flight out. I will call you later, okay?"

"Nikki, I love you. Call me as soon as you hear something."

"I will. Goodbye and kiss Alena for me."

The airport was a madhouse with crying babies and frantic people all trying to get out of New Orleans before the hurricane hit. I was ready to leave.

"Next."

"Hello, I would like to change my flight to leave out today, please."

"I am sorry, Ma'am," the soft spoken clerk said to me apologetically. "All flights are booked. Your flight is scheduled out tomorrow at 8:00am. We can place you on standby for today, but that means you will lose a guaranteed reservation for tomorrow and risk not getting a flight out at all. A standby means that you will be here for the next twelve-to-fourteen hours hoping for a flight." I was annoyed.

"I know what the fuck *stand-by* means. I just need to get home."

"You and everybody else, Ma'am."

An anxious gentleman in line, eager to get an outgoing flight almost seemed as if he wished that he could make the decision and purchase the ticket for my flight.

I sighed. "Okay, I will wait until tomorrow. I will go back to my hotel room and return tomorrow morning. Thank you very much. I apologize for my rudeness. I know that you are doing your best."

Returning to the hotel, I did not unpack my bags, but went through them to find something more comfortable. Although Allen was not happy with me still being in New Orleans, we both agreed that there was not much that we could do to prevent it.

I pulled my book out for some light reading and noticed that I still had Gayle's dildo and needed to return it. She obviously did not miss it, as it was never mentioned. When my knocks went unanswered, I entered into Gayle's room to return the dildo where I had located it. She still had a lot of packing left to do. As I rummaged to hide her dildo with the others, I noticed a letter addressed to Allen sitting atop her dresser. I read in disbelief, little words like, *'your wife and the Principal,' 'cheating,' 'undeserving of you,'* and *'late night,'* were written in a letter to Allen, telling him of her witnessing Craig coming from my hotel.

"What the hell are you doing?"

Startled, I immediately became angry when I saw her. Her guarded body language told me that she was afraid of what would happen but was prepared to defend herself.

"Gayle, you have thirty seconds to start talking before I tag your ass. How dare you write a letter to my husband about what you think you know!"

"Well, I saw him c-come out of the hotel," she stuttered. "And I just assumed that it was because he was w-with you and when you did not deny it—well, I just th-thought that meant you were g-guilty."

"Did I have to deny it, you jealous bitch? Do I owe your ass anything? Do you want my man, too? Are you trying to break and take my family?" I tightened my fist. "Do you think that my husband would want your butch ass, even if you did manage to break us up with your lies, Gayle?" I clenched the other fist.

For a moment, I had actually forgotten that I had been unfaithful. Or maybe I really believed that it was okay. Either way, I was ready to fight her after realizing that she had been sitting back hoping for me to sex Craig so that she could take my husband.

"Gayle, I knew that you were dirt, but I did not know you were *that* dirty."

She moved backwards while I moved toward her. "I am sorry, Nikki," she cowered. "I did not know that—"

Before she could finish, I began to pound her in the face, chest, and stomach. I was enraged. Although Gayle was significantly bigger than I, she did not have a chance to respond to the quickness of my movements.

My fury was openly unleashed and I continued to punch her face. I was suddenly pulled away from her. I continued flailing my arms and kicking until I realized who had me.

"Nikki! Gayle! What is going on?" It was Craig.

Out of breath, I could not speak. I began to sob as the seriousness of my actions of kicking my boss's ass, began to consume me. Gayle also began wail that she was sorry for accusing me of sleeping with Craig and writing the letter. He did not recoil and only laughed at Gayle, reminding her that there were more women in this building than me. He told her how ridiculous she was for writing a letter to my husband, based on speculation, and simply walked away.

Craig stopped by because he had rented a car to leave New Orleans. In spite of what the clerks promised, he did not believe that the airports would be flying out any aircrafts tomorrow due to the speed in which the hurricane was approaching. We loaded into the rental and joined the thousands of people waiting in traffic to get out of New Orleans. It took us almost two days to drive home from New Orleans, but Craig was right. No flights went out the next day and thousands of people were left stranded in New Orleans.

Before dropping Gayle at home, she continued to apologize for her behavior and begged for our forgiveness, hoping that it did not affect our work or personal relationships. *Too late for that*, I thought. I was happy to learn, however, that there would not be any repercussions for whipping her ass. I simply wanted her out of my space and apparently, so did Craig.

Before Craig took me home, he asked me to call Allen and tell him that I would be home within an hour or so, even though we were only ten minutes away. Craig and I checked into a Super 8 and had hard and deliberate sex for 45 minutes without speaking, only responding to how good our bodies made us feel when they came together as one. I was relieved to have him inside of me, riding his stallion. As I stared down at him, I drank in his soul with my eyes and breathed in his scent with my deepest inhalations. I did not want to forget the scent of him. As my body shuttered, he asked if he could keep me. I said yes and we made love once more before we left the room.

When we arrived home, Allen anxiously met us at the door with relief. I fell into his embrace and lost myself in his familiarity. Allen thanked Craig and they begin to discuss the hurricane. I quickly slipped away saying that I needed to bathe, thanked Craig for getting me and Gayle home then left the room. I joined Allen after showering with the news on showing how the levy had broken and that New Orleans was now under water. I cried in Allen's arms while watching. I cried for the residents, for the nice young desk clerk and because I missed Craig.

After returning to school a week later, the rumor mill was abuzz about Gayle transferring to a middle school across town. They bombarded me with questions wanting to know why. Reminding them that I was just returning from a two week hiatus, they seemed to get the picture that I was out of the loop and left me alone. I knew that within her heart, she knew that Craig and I were lovers in New Orleans.

Over time, Craig and I became creative in our meetings and mostly made love at school before anyone arrived or after everyone had gone home. Because my new office was off the beaten path, it was easy for us to have sex there without being detected. We did it as often as we could and maintained staunch professionalism throughout the work day. It was easy, especially since I knew that I would be getting my fill before I left for the day. I was addicted to the sheer rawness of our sex.

Without warning, Craig shut down. He became more and more distant toward me, blocked my calls, and my emails. Realizing that our affair was abruptly over was brutally hurtful. We would pass one another in the hallway with nothing more than a nod and that was only when we thought someone was watching. Otherwise, he would not even look my way. Passing by Stanley Jeffers office after staying late one day, I heard voices of what seemed like cries. As I quietly moved closer, I slightly pushed the door open and was so shocked that I had to cover my mouth to muffle the scream that was sure to escape had I not.

Stanley and Craig were embracing in a loving way. Stanley's hands were on Craig's lower back and their bodies were pressed against one another. There was intimacy and tears. There was caring and consolation. There was affection and tenderness. It was a scene right out of *Broke Back Mountain*. I was sick and stumbled away in disgust. A wave of nausea hit me with a blow that forced vomit as I shockingly concluded that Craig was on the down-low while he had been getting down low with me.

I was devastated. I had no one to call or cry out to as Gayle and I had not spoken since returning from New Orleans and no one else knew of my infidelity. I physically became ill and began to call in sick to avoid seeing Craig and Jeffers. The sight of them continued to creep into my mind, taunting me and making my stomach churn with disgust. This man, that I had now made love to countless numbers of times and lied to my husband for, was now my enemy. I replayed the times when I kissed, licked, and sucked on his manhood after it had been inside of a man's ass. I vomited again. I managed to convince Allen that I had the stomach flu which was why my stomach was so upset. Allen, being a certified germaphobe, allowed distance from him and Alena. I could not face either one of them right now. I simply wanted to be alone and cry.

After more than two weeks of absence, I returned to work to find a stack of papers on my desk and back logs to complete. Over the next few days, I buried myself in work, avoiding everyone as much as possible. I heard a soft knock on the door and I looked up to see the new head counselor, Mrs. Avery.

"Come in, please."

"Nikki, how are you feeling? I heard that you had one heck of a bug that kept you hanging off the side of the bed on a regular basis." Her eyes were full of genuine concern, so I began to relax and let my guard down a little. "Are you pregnant?" She asked quietly. *Nosey bitch*, I thought. *I would not tell you if I were.*

"Pregnant? Oh, no way. I just came down with something that would not let go of me. I am fine now plus I think that morning sickness lasts more than two weeks." Although the thought of pregnancy had never occurred to me before, it did now and I made a mental note to purchase a pregnancy test.

"Well, I wanted to update you on the latest news about Principal Craig," she said. My stomach immediately began to do cartwheels and I had to quickly drink water to keep the bubble of disgust from once again manifesting into upchuck. I positioned myself for the news that he and Mr. Jeffers had been discovered. "He has announced that he will be transferring back to California in two weeks. He did not give much reason other than he had to take care of a sick relative. The senior principal has recommended Mr. Jeffers as acting sixth grade Assistant Principal, since he worked so closely with Principal Craig and can fill in until a permanent replacement is found."

I felt relieved that I would no longer have to see Craig.

"Thanks for the news. I am sorry to hear that he is leaving so soon, Mrs. Avery. But I understand the importance of taking care of family."

"Yes, I am sure that you do." Lingering as if there was more, she continued. "Nikki, let's clear our schedules for lunch next week, as I have not had much of an opportunity to get to know you. I hear that you were specifically requested for this school due to your expertise with troubled youth. That says a lot about your character and your skills." We agreed to have lunch next week. "Have a great rest of the week. Don't stay here too late trying to catch up. You have all week to do that."

As the school began to empty and quietness settled around me, I called the security desk to let them know that I was still in the building and requested a walkie-talkie. They agreed to bring one down shortly. The cramping in my stomach from throughout the day seemed to intensify. So, I decided to work just a few minutes longer then head home to Allen. As I heard footsteps getting closer, I raised my head to greet the security guard, but to my surprise, it was not the security guard at all.

"Hello Mrs. Raye."

"Hello," I said, as I sat back and waited. *Jeffers.* I was not happy to see him.

"I know that you are surprised to see me but I have been waiting for you to return so I that could share some things with you."

"I have already heard the news, so that will not be necessary." I just wanted him gone.

"Please allow me to finish, as you have not heard this news," he said snidely.

Wondering where the hell that security guard was, a feeling of uneasiness began to settle over me and I searched for anything to protect myself in the event that things escalated out of control.

"I know about the affair," he began. I did not respond. "I know about the trip to New Orleans and about the numerous times you had sex in this office, in his car, and wherever else you decided to spread your nastiness."

The silence was so loud that the sound made my head ache. I was staring at this person who had, over the months, watched me with a competitive hatred. I had no idea that we were not only sharing the same lover, but the same disgust for one another.

He continued.

"The argument that day was about his interest in you, you know? I wanted to know why he could not make up his mind as to whether or not he wanted me or you. I was so angry that I threatened to lie and expose a relationship that had yet to exist, if he did not make a decision. It seems that my ultimatum backfired because he encouraged me to do it, but I could not." *Thank God,* I thought.

"I knew from the moment that he laid eyes on you that he would not stop until he had you. He orchestrated the entire trip to New Orleans for the sake of you, but was surprised when the senior principal decided that Gayle should accompany you to New Orleans instead of him. I managed to convince the senior principal to allow me to accompany Craig to D.C. It was my hope to rebuild our failing relationship since moving to Atlanta." Surprised, I was finally able to speak.

"Prior to your moving to Atlanta?" I asked.

"Yes Nikki. He was my lover in California, also. We secretly lived together there and we lived together here. You are such a stupid woman. Did you not see the signs?"

Moving closer into my space, he continued. "Didn't you ever wonder why you always had to meet at hotels or go out of town? He told you that he was single, so it should have been easy for you to lay together at his place, right? You were so taken by his beauty and charm that you would rather spend time anywhere than to argue. He knew that. Don't feel too bad, as the same thing happened to me before we became committed, but his storyline was a little more complicated then. He simply never shared it until we moved here."

As I sat mortified and terrified at the eerie calmness of this man, I tightened my grip on the can of mace that I had managed to grab from my bag, ready to spray it if he moved any closer. Jeffers continued to block the door while searching my expressionless face for a trace of acknowledgement. Even though my brain was spinning, I was not about to give that punk the satisfaction of seeing me squirm.

"Mr. Jeffers, I think that you should leave now."

He ignored my request and in his most whiney voice said, "I have pictures of you and Craig having sex in your office, you know? You and Craig were so into one another that you never even saw me watching. But, that is another story. Let's get back to the matter at hand, shall we?" My mind began to scatter. *Did he say pictures? Oh hell no. I am going to have to take this bitch down before he does something that I cannot reverse.*

"I know what you are thinking," he said. "Don't worry about the pictures. I eventually deleted them because I did not want to hurt Craig. Well, I deleted most of them." I am not believing that this sneaky little white waif of a man is threatening me because I took his bitch.

"Nikki, when Craig left D.C. during the middle of the conference, I did a little sleuthing and found out that he had gone to New Orleans. I also caught a flight the same day. It was not difficult locating you, as it was the clerk at the hotel who told me that most locals end up at the Blues Café and it's within walking distance. When I saw you talking to that lesbian, I almost thought that this might be a break for me. While watching you, I also noticed Craig entering the bar just as the lady punched your prospective date."

"She was not my date, bitch! Getting down with the same sex is your thing, not mine. I can't believe you brought your punk ass in here to tell me what? That you saw me? What the fuck? You still got your man, so what is the problem? Are you mad because he is leaving you too? Take your bitch ass back with him. Then you will be certain to have him to yourself." I was livid.

Jeffers stepped back as if I were going to attack him, yet he never stopped talking. "I made my way to Craig at the club and he quickly led me away."

I suddenly realized that I did see Jeffers that night, but did not know that he was there looking for Craig.

"Craig convinced me that his visit would be short-lived as he was unexpectedly asked to speak at the conference and that I needed to go back to D.C. He showed me his return flight ticket and assured me that he would be in D.C. by 5pm, the next day. We made love in my room shortly afterwards. I fell asleep in his arms but awakened to an empty bed."

I began to feel queasy just picturing Craig taking it up the rear or giving it. Even worse, he came to me after making love to a man. It was unnatural and I simply wanted to die right where I stood. Jeffers continued.

"Craig did not return as promised, so I knew that he was probably sharing a bed with you by then. He did not return my calls and eventually turned off his cell phone. The next time that I talked to him was the night that the three of you returned home.

"He had your sex on his body when he returned home and it made me sick to my stomach," he said.

Made you sick? I thought.

"I insisted that Craig get tested for STD's, because I felt that this was probably not your first time being unfaithful and I did not want your trash."

"My *trash?* You fuck men, Jeffers," I said, pointing at him. "You take it up the ass! But *you* call *me* trash! Frankly, I am the one who should get tested after sexing behind the two of you!" Crying angrily, I was ready to fight.

"Yes, Nikki, you should because—" The ringing phone startled the both of us. It was the security guard telling me that my husband was on his way to my office. Surprised that Allen was here, I asked security to tell him to remain at the desk as I was packing up now.

Before hanging up, I sarcastically thanked him for the bringing the walkie-talkie.

"Jeffers, I have to leave because your putrid punk stench is making me nauseous." Unmoved, he replied, "Anyway, give me just five more minutes and I will not bother you any further." Not sure if I wanted to hear anymore, I stood to hear the last. "As I was saying, you need to get tested because both mine and Craig's test results came back positive for the HIV".

Floored, I fell back into my seat and watched Jeffers give an evil grin of pleasure. My body tightened and I could not breathe. I was paralyzed with this knowledge of certain death. The tears began to roll but words would not surface.

"Yes. I was surprised, too. The irony is that I insisted that Craig get tested but I am the one with the virus. That is some sick shit, right? Craig has been my lover for over seven years, Nikki, and dying with him will be a pleasure." He bowed. I raised my head, eyes so full of tears that Jeffers' face was blurred.

"I have but one question for you, Nikki."

"Yes?"

"Who's the *bitch* now?" He walked out.

The phone rang again but I could not bring myself to answer and soon heard footsteps ascend upon me. When the door opened, I was relieved to see that it was my husband and fell into his comforting embrace.

With the realization that I possibly had HIV, I lied to Allen and said that I had a yeast infection to avoid his advances. I eventually convinced him to wear a condom, citing that I did not want to risk transmittance.

He understood and we began to make love with a lie and a condom between us.

"Mommy, I am so excited about my birthday party," squealed Alena. Jumping on her trampoline,
"I am a big girl, now."

"Yes, you are, Alena, and Mommy is so proud of you." As I hugged my beautiful daughter, I could not help but to wonder if I would live to see her grow up. I decided not to get tested right away and tried to live my life as normal as possible. Educated, yet fallen prey to an ignorant fear of HIV, I drank and ate from disposable cups and utensils. I washed my clothes separately and changed my toothbrush often. I removed myself from any activity that could possibly spread the virus to my family including eventual intimacy with Allen.

"Mommy!" My thoughts were broken by Alena's screams. She had fallen off the trampoline and deeply gashed the side of her body on broken glass. We rushed her to the hospital and were told that she would need a blood transfusion. Allen's compromised family history prompted fear and he insisted that I become the primary donor and he secondary. As they prepped me for the transfusion, I was ashamed because I was willing to risk the life of my daughter to conceal my infidelity.

I told Allen that I could not go through with it because I was afraid. I asked him to get the doctor and use the blood that was in the blood bank or his own. Allen grew angry.

"Why would you want to risk giving our child potentially diseased blood when you are the perfect match?!" Although irrational, Allen was terribly afraid of any germs and the thought of giving Alena the blood of a stranger was overwhelming. "Get over yourself just this one time to save our baby!" Calming himself, Allen softens his approach. "Look, Nikki, Alena needs you to help her pull through this. You can do it, baby. I know that you can." I began to cry.

When Allen left the room, I asked for the doctor and told him that my lover was diagnosed with HIV and that I may have been infected but had not gotten tested. The doctor moved quickly and sent the nurse to the blood bank. Allen, wondering what just happened, was ushered down the hallway as the doctor began to explain what just happened. He could only look over at me in disgust and then he looked away.

Alena was out of surgery and recovering in ICU. After taking my blood test, I cautiously walked to the window to look in on Alena. She looked so vulnerable. I could not believe that I almost risked the life of my flesh and blood to save a marriage that I no longer deserved and a reputation that was already lost. I immediately wanted my family back but knew they were gone. God was now teaching me that lesson. Allen would not look at me directly, but I felt his stares on my back as I watched Alena.

I heard him tell the nurses to not allow me to go inside as I might have AIDS *ignorance* and he did not want to risk our daughter with her cuts and bruises being exposed. The nurse explained that Alena was safe in my presence and that I could not be denied the right to see her. I wanted to scream that I was sorry. I wanted him to hold me and say that everything would be okay. But he did not. He could not. I was dead to him, at least for this very moment.

I needed to escape the deafening silence and unspoken accusations, but could not leave Alena, so I went to the hospital chapel to pray. The serenity and beauty of the chapel was calming. Other than myself, only one other person was there. As I sat and prayed in silence for Alena's recovery, I felt a touch on my shoulder. Allen had forgiven me after all, I thought. But as I turned around, I was met by a kind faced man with soft blue eyes.

"May I pray with and for you, my sister?"

"Yes, please," I said.

"Is there something specific that you would like for me to pray for?"

"Please pray for a speedy recovery for my little girl, Alena, who is in ICU. The doctors seem to think that she will be fine, but a word to the Father never hurts, right?"

"Right, you are. Is there anything else, the Pastor asked? I noticed earlier that your husband was by your side and now you are apart. This is not the time for separation, as your daughter needs you both by her side. Shall I get him for you?"

"No", thank you. I am the last person that he would like to see right now. I have really hurt him and my family."

"I betrayed his trust and I don't think that even he will ever forgive me. And even if he does forgive me, I can never forgive myself," I sobbed. He prayed for me and never asked another question. He just allowed me to receive his prayers and cry.

I wept for many days. Alena arrived home one week after the accident and both Allen and I channeled all of our energy toward her and away from one another. He had not spoken to me since discovering my infidelity. I received a call earlier that day that my test results were back and that I needed to stop by Dr. Fitzgerald's office today. I decided to wait until the next day since it was

Alena's first day home. Allen mostly handled her needs, as it was an unspoken known that until the results were in, both he and Alena were off limits to me.

I arrived at Dr. Fitzgerald's office the next morning bright and early. It seemed as if I waited an eternity before his arrival. I was prepared for the worst and had made certain that all of my life insurance policies were paid up and that my supplemental insurance would continue even if I no longer worked for the school district. I had taken a leave of absence and did not know if I would return based on Alena's recovery and my pending diagnosis.

I wiped my hands onto my jeans to keep the moisture away, but the moisture kept returning. My throat was dry and I was finding it difficult to breathe and sit still. After today, my life would change for the better or worse. Either way, it would change.

"Good morning Nikki. Let's get right to it, okay? Your test results are negative. You do not have HIV. This does not mean that you are clear for the virus as it has an incubation period that requires monitoring but as of right now, all is well."

It had been almost nine months since my last contact with Craig, so things looked positive. He would test me again in three months.

I fell to my knees in prayer and then drove home to share the news with Allen, but he and Alena were gone. The letter read that he does not want to know the circumstances surrounding my probability of contracting HIV, because if it were an honest mistake, I would have shared that information immediately and probably would have asked for help for the sake of our family. But since I did not, he suspected that cheating was involved and did not want to hear of my infidelity with another man. He wrote that he simply wanted to move forward with his and Alena's life, no matter the results of my test. He closed stating that an attorney would be in touch.

"Allen!" I screamed. "Allen!" I cried. But Allen was gone. Like a mad woman, I ran from room to room calling "Alena!" Allen!" But my calls went unanswered. I snapped. I began breaking, throwing and tearing everything that I could get my hands on.

Pictures of me and Allen were smashed. Expensive lamps and vases, shattered. China and crystal, crushed. I slashed curtains, beat holes into the walls with hammers and threw chairs until I was exhausted and defeated. I wanted to die, but I was too much of a coward to do it myself, so I just cried until sleep seized my exhaustion and rocked me into a traumatized slumber for days.

I was awakened by multiple knocks at the door and the doorbell ringing. Someone was calling my name.

"Nikki, are you in there?" When I recognized the voice, I struggled to the door and collapsed into Gayle's arms. *The one woman who tried to break my marriage,* I thought, *is now seeking redemption in the form of a personal rescue.* I was too weak to help myself and allowed her to help me. Gayle ran my bath and helped me into the tub. While soaking, I heard her sweeping glass and vacuuming. When she thought that I had finished bathing, she helped me from the tub, dried and clothed me.

"Nikki, you need to eat something."

"How did you know?" I asked.

"Lisa called and told me about Alena's accident. When I could not contact you, I called Allen and he shared with me what was going on with you and that you might need help. He told me that he had taken Alena and was going to try and move forward with his life. He said that he thinks you cheated on him."

"Were you all too happy to confirm it, Gayle?" I asked sarcastically. "Since he is such a good man, maybe you came over here to see what my test results were so that you can see what your chances are with him."

"I guess I deserved that, Nikki. I did not tell Allen that you cheated because you told me you did not. Obviously, you lied because here you are."

Shifting uneasily, I continued to listen. "For the record, I would have never given Allen the letter. I was venting and I just wrote it out of anger. You were right about Sneed. He lasted a hot minute with me and left me in record time for another woman who was from New Orleans. Anyway, I did some asking around after I received a call from Lisa and found out about Craig."

"Did you know that he was a punk, Gayle?" Gayle's mouth moved, but no words surfaced. "Yes, Craig is a punk and his girlfriend's name is Stanley Jeffers. You were right about him."

Stunned, Gayle still could not speak. I continued. "After I found out that Craig was moving, Jeffers cornered me and told me that he and Craig were lovers and had been for years. I probably would not have believed him if I had not seen them hugged up with my own eyes. They are both punks, but only one of them was on the down low."

"Jeffers told me that Craig moved back to California because he found out that both he and Jeffers were positive and that I should get checked, also. That is the real deal, Gayle. When I could not help Alena, I had to say why and that is how Allen found out. I am a lying, stinking bitch and I deserve this from Allen. I deserve it."

"Nikki, are you positive?"

"No, I am not and it has almost been ten months since our last encounter. Dr. Fitzgerald seems to think that I am in the clear now, but I have to get tested in three months just to be sure. Gayle, I have never been so afraid in my life. If I ever get Allen back, I will never cheat again."

I did not get Allen back. Even though my test results remained negative, Allen did not come back to me. We spoke only through attorneys and eventually divorced with shared custody of Alena, who now lives with me. I did not return to school from my personal leave. I received my doctorate shortly thereafter and started a home based e-counseling business.

I did, however, remain in contact with Mrs. Avery, who informed me that Mr. Jeffers had fallen ill and was no longer at the middle school. I assumed that his illness was now taking hold of his immune system. The most surprising news was that Craig moved back home to his wife and kids and now had another child on the way.

There was never an ailing family member, but a wife who needed her husband and kids who needed their father. It also turned out that Jeffers was the only one who was infected and used his sickness to seal the break up between me and Craig. It seems that Craig obviously opted to do something with Jeffers that he did not with me which was to practice safe sex. I can only surmise that what I witnessed was two lovers saying goodbye after one realized that he tested positive or because the other realized that home was where he was most needed. I will never know. It only makes sense now why Craig had to distance himself not only from me but Jeffers.

I have called Craig's new school often but could never find the words to say hello, goodbye or fuck you. I sometimes still want to be in his life, in his space, and even feel his body. I can now relate to, but not truly understand, why women stay with their men once it is discovered that they are on the down low.

Before moving to the next chapter, write down some thoughts that you would like to discuss later. Explain why you feel this way.

Raw Addiction II (BJ's Story)

Chapter 2

Adjusting to life as a single woman now is sometimes overwhelmingly lonely. This morning, however, I decided to stop feeling sorry for myself and spend time reconnecting socially, beginning with a little retail therapy. The shopping reduced my stress level as I perused the racks to find something sexy to compliment my cocoa skin tone and taut body. Softly draped in my favorite ethnic summer dress, my locs had now grown out past my shoulders blades, where they rest lightly.

My natural aura of peace kept my mind at ease when it drifted back to the repulsion of having a bi-sexual ex-lover and the sadness and loss of my now my ex-husband. My soul quietly suggested that I find a place for it to live without complications and I promised to oblige.

The meeting was innocent enough, I suppose. Not really noticing him, but acknowledging his presence, I continued forward with my thoughts of affirmations. He circled my space like a shark, checking my form, while clearly trying to determine the best way to attack.

Flattered, I pretended not to notice the beauty of his smile and the uncertainty of his stance. He was mentally positioning himself for rejection but hoping for acceptance. Feeling confident yet a little unsure myself, I smiled a welcoming hello and watched his body slip into a state of unconscious relaxation. He introduced himself but I heard not a word. He was gorgeous, from the top of his head to the soles of his expensive shoes.

I acknowledged every word that was verbalized and found myself agreeing to dinner. Close enough to inhale the scent of his cologne, I began to envision my lips on his small, yet full lips and imagined the feeling of pressing my body close to his. I immediately wanted the full view. In comparison to my past men, he was short in stature. There was an uncomplicated honesty about him that I was willing to invest in. His conversation disclosed intelligence. He appeared, on the surface, my scholarly equal and promised stimulating conversation, which would be a welcomed change from the silence that I roomed currently housed.

As I prepared for our date, my mind crept back to Craig. This thought process was perplexing because I still loved him in spite of everything and often longed for his touch. Interrupting my thoughts, my phone buzzed. The text read, *"I can't wait to see you."* It from was BJ.

"You won't be disappointed," I replied.

Looking through the closet trying to decide on which dress to wear, the doorbell rang.

"What now? Who is it?" I yelled.

"Girl, if you do not open this freaking door, you will know once I kick this mofo in." It was Tina, my brutally honest, over protective, self-proclaimed big sister. She was a chore sometimes, but I loved her dearly. As I looked through the peephole, a big brown eyeball stared back.

"Whore, open the door," she laughingly fussed. Unlocking the door, she entered with an audible force.

"How you gone just go out with somebody you just met? What do you know about him, Nikki? He could be a bad-ass or a con-artist or child molester, some shit like that. I want his cell phone, his home phone, his friend's phonc, his address and his driver's license number. Oh and his Momma's number."

She was on a roll. "And his credit history! Look, I know you trying to get over that punk of yours and you just went through a divorce and all, but damn, you need to slow your roll. You are my girl. I couldn't stand your ass at first, but love the hell out of you and Alena, so you need to make certain that this guy is cool."

A ball of fire, Tina and I were once neighbors. When Allen and I moved to a different part of Georgia, we lost touch for a while and rarely visited. Before starting my own business, I saw Tina at an educators meeting and we rekindled our friendship. It was the best medicine in my recovery from Craig and Allen, as Tina had an opinion about everything that was happening in my life. The truth be told, she needed to focus on her own house but I would not tell her that.

"What is the name of the restaurant?" Tina asked. "I am not saying that I am going to drive by, but a sista wanna know." Stopping to pause, we looked at one another and burst into laughter.

"You are my girl and you got my fucking back for real!", hugging her.

Being the candid person that she is, Tina mentioned that my dress selection was nice but my shoes were not on point.

"Girl, I know that you are not trying to show those twenty-five, slave-walking toes on a first date. You'd better hide those mugs under some extra-long slacks or closed toe pumps." We both folded over and cracked up in laughter again. She was right. My toes were jacked up and if I wanted to impress BJ, the open toe pumps will have to wait until I impressed him with my other body parts. Once composed, she poured two glasses of wine and we conversed as I reapplied my makeup.

"BJ is a nice man", Tina. "He is a much needed distraction from the ex-hubby and Craig. I need that Tina," I pleaded. "He seems genuinely interested in me."

"Since Craig left, I have been very sad and lonely. I have lost myself. I lost my lover. I lost my husband, and came close to losing my child. I really need this date."

"Why did you say you lost your lover before your husband, Nikki?"

Shrugging my shoulders, I did not have an answer. At least not one that I wanted to share. I missed Craig still but could not tell Tina how much he still lived inside my heart. She would not understand.

As if reading my mind, Tina replied, "Sis, you know that I understand. Hell, I am in a well-we-in-it-now marriage. I sometimes cry at night and work out in the mornings, all the while trying to maintain the equilibrium of a balanced life. Who, more than I, understand?" Sitting in silence and reflecting on her own personal problems, Tina finally said, "Well, enough of the pity party, tell me all about him."

I slid the phone across the table to show a picture.

"What the hell is that?" She asked. "That is the biggest dick that I have ever seen! Oh my goodness!"

Smirking through the silence of Tina's surprise, I waited. I did not mind her seeing a picture of his manhood because I did not have any real intentions of seeing BJ on a committed level. Plus I just had to share the vision of dick wealth with my girl.

"Arc you there, Tina?" I snapped my fingers.

"Girl, I am still staring at this dick pic. How does a sista swallow deep throat without choking?"

"I have not gotten there yet, but I will let you know", I winked.

After a few more drinks and saying goodbye, I decided to peruse the internet in search of the real Brian James before his arrival, as where there is one dick-pic, there usually are many others. He was seemingly on every social media site possible, including the ones that would allow him to showcase his manhood!

Is he a wanna-be porn star? Opting to not immediately tell Tina what I discovered, I decided that after our date tonight, I would ask probing questions to find out just exactly who Brian "BJ" James, really is.

We had never been on an actual date but had experienced several sessions of hot phone sex so I was looking forward to the real thing. Wearing my best Victoria Secrets bra and panties, I sprayed a floral scent between my 36DD breasts and between my thighs to make sure that the freshness was covering both ends. Checking my slim frontal and side booty physique in the mirror for one last approving time, the doorbell rang breaking my thoughts of admiration.

Looking at my watch, I realized that BJ was early. *Hmmmm,* I thought, *He can't wait.* I looked through the peephole and stopped breathing for a second. *Why is he here?* I thought. *Should I even open the door?* My heartbeat was pounding erratically strong throughout my chest.

"I just want to talk, Nikki," he spoke. "I know you are inside. Please forgive me for just showing up." I slowly opened the door and Allen stood before me. He was thinner but still handsome. I had not physically seen him since the divorce.

Outside of speaking on the phone, we agreed that Alena would be picked up and dropped off at Mom's during hours of visitation and it worked out for the both of us. He was rarely a passing thought these days and his name was only mentioned when Alena or Mom said it.

After the affair with Craig, I attempted to contact Allen to apologize for the hurt that I had caused. He refused to speak with me about anything, except Alena, while our divorce and child custody proceedings were pending. Allen and I agreed to share custody of Alena, with my being the primary custodian of our daughter. Regardless of what happened between us, Allen shared his beliefs with the court that infidelity does not make an unfit mother, only an unfit wife. I concurred and Alena was given back to me.

Allen stopped by only fifteen minutes before BJ was to schedule to arrive. Curious about his visit, I allowed Allen inside, in hopes that he would leave within fifteen minutes. Allen has always been a gentleman and I, in no way, felt threatened by him. I could feel Allen's eyes taking in my round ass and long legs, which were accentuated by my five-inch heels, as we walked to sit down.

"You look very nice," he said.

"Are you and Gayle going out tonight?" That was his way of asking if I was seeing anyone. I avoided the question.

"What's going on, Allen? Why are you here?" Shifting slightly, Allen softly grabbed my hand and began to share a conversation that he and Alena had.

"Alena wants her parents back together, Nikki. She tells me often, whenever the two of us are together, how nice it would be if Mommy was here and I must that I have missed you, as well."

"Please know that I have long since forgiven you for everything that happened in the past and have been seeing a therapist to help me resolve my feelings of resentment toward you. The therapist has helped me to see that I am entitled to my feelings, but must also move past them to heal. This healing process includes accepting your apology. I do, Nikki, accept your apology".

As I continued to sit quietly, listening to my ex-husband accept my apology for cheating, lying, and scheming, my body slightly softened towards him and for a moment, I was accepting of his words and the genuine love that he expressed for what could be again.

Until this moment, I had never considered Allen as a potential mate again but the possibilities were certainly there. My feelings for him have been in hibernation but slowly began to rise. As I grabbed his other hand, the doorbell rang. I did not move. The doorbell rang again. I still did not move. As Allen's eyes met mine, he held the gaze but slowly dropped my hands, moving towards the door. I stood. I heard greetings, introductions, and the door closing. Still standing, BJ emerged.

Without words, he circled my body then stood in back of me. Moving the zipper downward, my dress fell to the floor. Laying me down on the sofa, BJ forced his face between my legs, forcing my body to jerk uncontrollably within minutes. My brain was not connecting to what was happening to my vagina. For the first time in my life, not even with Craig, had I ever experienced a type orgasm that shook me from the core of my body, inside out. I never thought of Allen again.

I was hooked, wanted a relationship, and BJ knew it. Knowing that BJ was not yet ready to settle down from the single life, I allowed him to move into my home anyway. Immediately, the cohabitation became stressful as I suffered through BJ weaning himself from several women with whom he was sexting and probably sexing, too. With each discovery, he would remind me that he was still in a single state of mind but did not want to lose the beautiful love that had grown between us and that he simply needed more time to become the man that I needed for him to become. He was shelving me. Still suffering from trust issues, I wanted to believe that he was sincere in his efforts and refused to lose in love again. Especially, since I was now pregnant with his child.

We argued often. I was determined to keep him in my world for the sake of our growing family. I used the only weapon that I felt I owned against his weakness, which was my ability to create sexual fantasies. After preparing a great meal for us, we sat down to watch TV.

"Great dinner, babe," BJ said while pulling me close and rubbing my rounding stomach. I snuggled into him and began to stroke his penis. "Hey, take a break," he said, pushing my hand away. Feeling rejected, I choked back tears.

"What's wrong?"

"There is nothing wrong." He reached over me to grab the laptop. "I've got something to work on before work tomorrow. We can take this up later." I didn't believe him.

"But we are supposed to be watching a movie".

Unmoved and ignoring me, he continued to open the laptop and log on. I watched the movie alone while he sat beside me working.

"Babe, the movie is off," I said drowsily. "Let's go to bed." I stood to leave. He didn't move.

"Are you coming? We can shower together."

Shaking his head no but promising to shower with me tomorrow, I glanced at his laptop screen, where he seemed fully engaged in researching stocks and bonds.

Becoming both tired and frustrated waiting for BJ to come to bed in hopes of experiencing his tasty goodness, I became angry that he did not want to be with me and stormed off into the bedroom. Laying quietly and sulking, I vaguely heard sexual sounds. I tiptoed across the room and slowly opened the bedroom door and saw BJ masturbating to a threesome on his computer screen.

"What the fuck are you doing?" I demanded. "You'd rather fuck your hands than me? Seriously!" Humiliated and insulted, I grabbed his laptop and threw it onto the floor, breaking it.

Without saying a word, BJ pulled me close to him, forcing me to be still. As I struggled, his grip became tighter. Heaving and drained, I stopped fighting and relaxed my body into him, sobbing.

"I'm sorry for doing this to you. Yes, I purposely waited you out to watch porn. I am addicted and want to watch it often. I love posting pictures of my dick for everyone to see. I love women. I love everything about them and before you, I sexed them all, anytime and anywhere. The women in Atlanta are a dime a dozen and will give it up for free just to have someone hold them." I sat sobbing and listening.

"You came into my life like a whirlwind, trying to jack a brother up and strip him down of his life and his chicks. You are a good woman and I jumped into this lifestyle with you so that I could keep tabs on you and prevent some other dude getting you. I know it's not right but I also know that you are the best person for me. So, will you please work with me? I will shut everything down, right now—every website and social media outlet."

This time, I did not have any words only more tears. I cried because he was honest and I knew how difficult it was for him to share this harsh truth with me. Even though I did not like how I learned of his addiction to porn, I decided that my expertise as a Clinical Psychologist would benefit both him and myself as there was clearly something deeper there. Over the months, I learned more than I ever wanted to know about BJ and it changed the course of our relationship. Although we became closer, we also experienced a distance. We stayed together and became friends for the first time.

"Babe, are you ready?" I asked.

BJ and I had established a rapport throughout those difficult truths that ultimately resulted in marriage just before our son was born. Married life with him was acceptingly pretentious and we now lived in our own version of acceptable unhappiness. As we prepared to go out for New Year's Eve, I reflected on how our lives had grown individually and was appreciative enough for the struggle to keep us together.

"You look good, babe. I love the way that dress is hugging that ass."

I had to agree that our son had left me with a great bonus of even larger breasts and an extra round ass, which caught the eyes of many. My locs had grown impressively and cascaded down my back like a strong waterfall. I was content with my new self, as I kissed my mirror's image, leaving a soft red imprint of my full lips on its face, before closing the door behind me.

Atlanta's Velvet Room was filled to capacity with chicks in the shortest tightest dresses. They showcased bare legs and backs, long weaves, fake eyelashes, and high heels. There were beautiful women all around in various shapes, sizes, and ethnicities but none that rivaled me. I felt confident, sexy, and beautiful. Thanks to a hook up from BJ's cousin Bo, who was a bouncer at the club, we were ushered to the VIP section upon arrival. Checking the hatred and level of envy in the eyes of the women, I immediately stood taller and stronger, reaffirming my position as the "baddest chick" in the building.

I heard my name and turned with attitude to see my good friend, Tina. "Girl, stop fronting and act like you know me. Shit, can a sista get in VIP?"

"Hell yes!" We hugged and I pulled her into the VIP section along with her husband.

"Hey, BJ! Happy New Year!" Already tipsy, Tina was a welcomed sight and looked great in her blazing red cat-suit.

"Girl, I see your camel toe," I said. We both laughed and pointed to it, bubbling our lips like a camel. The atmosphere was festive and people were happy.

BJ excused himself to get us refills and to go for a smoke with Tina's husband, which left us a moment to chat. Before we even had a chance to converse, a beautiful male creature stood front and center. We both stared in awe.

"What's up, Jacobs?" Addressing me by my new last name, Tina knew immediately that he and I were familiar with one another, so I avoided eye contact in spite of her staring a hole through the side of my face.

"I saw your man leave, so I decided to take a moment to just say hello. It's been a minute. You look damn good in that dress. I peeped you as soon as you walked in, owning this bitch. I just wanted to let you know that I'm still interested and not just because that dress is hugging your ass. I remember."

Sobering us both up, we watched as Wright Reynolds walked away and out the door.

"Damn," Tina said. "He didn't even look at me and I'm light skinned!"

Before moving to next chapter, write down some thoughts that you would like to discuss later. Explain why you feel this way.

Raw Wrighteousness (A Naughty Bit)

Chapter 3

New Year's came to pass but I could not get Wright Reynolds out of my every waking thought. Thankful that BJ returned before Tina could probe that night, I promised to tell her everything about him the next day. Instead, I turned my phone off to avoid not answering her calls so that I could think about him uninterrupted.

I met Wright Reynolds at Chesapeake Middle School, where I had accepted a temporary assignment as the school Psychologist. It was refreshing to return to the familiarity of the education world with students and teachers alike. I walked into my office to find someone setting up the computer system.

"Hello."

Without looking up, he responded, "I will be out of your way very soon. I'm almost finished. I was hoping to have everything finished before you arrived but I was needed elsewhere."

Still talking to what appeared to be a very muscular back and shoulders, I introduced myself.

"My name is Nicole Jacobs. I am the new school Psychologist."

He turned slightly to acknowledge my presence and I was immediately gripped with nervousness when our eyes met. He was stunningly handsome with the sharpest cheekbones that I had ever seen. He was a tinge lighter than charcoal briquette with teeth as white as paint. His lined hair cut supported deep waves of softness. I thought, *He must have Indian in his blood*, and giggled as that is what black folk reference as the source of "good" hair.

"Did I say something to amuse you?"

Raising to stand, he stopped just short of my forehead. *Damn, where is the rest of his little short ass?* I thought. *He needs to keep raising up.*

Realizing that everyone had shortcomings, Wright Reynolds' was literally in his height. He was shorter than BJ but had a deliciously toned body tucked underneath that fitted shirt and jeans which looked hard and strong. He was a dapper and sexy little man who wore his silent confidence as if he was a six feet tall. He had dark, full lips that shield a big smile. I started to squirm. He extended his hand.

"My name is Wright Reynolds and you are all set. Please let me know if I can assist you further. I am just a radio call away. Welcome."

Not waiting for a response, he walked away and left me standing, slightly heated. We were very formal initially, but as the comfort levels increased, so did the attraction and inappropriate flirting, texting, sexting and eventually, touching. He was unhappily married and so was I. The bonding over unhappy moments with our spouses became our happiest times. Throughout the days, I found myself waiting for him to casually pass by my office for a quick hello followed by a hug and kiss behind closed doors. Recognizing that a pattern was forming yet again, I decided to cool things down and willingly shared the reason why this special friendship had to end.

I invested all of my energy into making the marriage work with BJ after my small filing. With his birthday coming soon, I decided to plan a party and called Tina over for party ideas and drinks.

"Girl, I ain't interested in planning no damn birthday party for him. Shit, all he does is hurt your heart and give you excuses why he won't give you none. You are always going out and buying sexy lingerie for him that he doesn't appreciate because he's never home. And when he is home, he still ain't home."

"Tina, just stop," I said. "I know that you don't like BJ, but he's really been having a tough time, feeling less than a man since he lost his job. He's depressed."

"He ain't that damn depressed if he's going to clubs and taking trips out of town with his unemployment check while you're struggling to pay the mortgage," Tina huffed.

"See that's why I don't tell your ass nothing because you always holding on to it and judging. I was angry when I shared that with you, Tina, and now you are throwing it back into my face?" I opened my laptop to research party ideas. "You know what Tina, I don't need your help. I will research the information myself."

"Good, I will pour the wine."

Pausing, I turned to look at her with a raised eyebrow.

"What? You thought I was leaving just because I told you about your man?" She turned up her glass. "Nope, I am going to drink this glass of wine and watch you do the work."

"I can't stand your ass, Tina."

"And I can't stand your ass, either."

Researching party ideas turned out to be more of a task than I bargained for. BJ's email and IM was open so I decided to look through his search engine for possible party ideas but found nothing.

An instant message pops up.

`LIDA001:"Round two?"`

I was not exactly sure what I was reading, but I felt my heart's palpitations increase. I stared at the screen not knowing how to respond. So I did not.

"Come look at this, Tina."

Our eyes met with an acknowledgement that those two words would most assuredly mean the end of my world with BJ. Although not confirmed, I would no longer allow BJ to rule over my existence with his dishonesty and cheating.

Without confronting BJ about yet another infidelity, I considered my marriage with him over and used that an as excuse to call Wright Reynolds. He immediately invited me to meet him at a small apartment on the outskirts of Atlanta. I looked fabulous in my short skirt and heels and knew for certain what would happen tonight. I was excited. Anticipating my arrival, the door opened without my even knocking. Without saying a word, Wright softly guided me into a candle lit room where a table was clothed with two covered plates and two wine filled glasses.

My heart raced and my palms began to moisten. Still not speaking but motioning for me to sit, I obediently followed his directive. Sitting across from each other in silence was more than my psyche could handle and a nervous giggle escaped. *Oh my God. Why the hell am I always giggling around this man? He is going to think I am a bubble head.* I composed myself and once again attempted to look into those piercing eyes. *Chile', this man is fine.*

He raised his glass to toast. "Here's to leaving monogamy screaming." The Psychologist in me was chomping at the bits to ask him, *"Why the hell you wanna say some shit like that and ruin a sista's cheating mood?"* I began to surmise that maybe he could possibly be speaking of himself. I really didn't need or want to know if this was his first time getting some strange. I did not want to be any grown ass man's first cheat.

"Too much pressure," I spoke aloud.

"Too much pressure from what?" He asked.

"Of being a nigga's first. I don't want to get all tangled up in someone else's feelings. I've got enough shit going on." Turning up my glass and drinking until empty, I slammed my glass down in frustration.

"I did not want conversation. Shit. I just wanted to get it and get the hell on."

"You have too simple a thought process for such an educated mind," he said quietly.

"Nigga, what?!"

Lifting his hand to silence me and my being too damned shocked that he was bold enough to say or do that, I stood to walk out.

"Monogamy is a persuasive state of interpretation," he began. "Within the institution of marriage, we teach people how to both treat us and how to think they need us. Where marriage defends the ideal of lifelong partnership, monogamy merely accepts it. My toast to leave monogamy screaming was a way of no longer accepting—"

Before he could finish his sentence, I was on him like a rabid dog. He was not only beautiful but also intelligent. Now I just wanted to see what he was working with. Pushing me away from him, I fell to the floor, legs spread open, exposing my nakedness.

Stunned, I lay there embarrassed while he just looked at me, expressionless.

Seconds passed before either one of us moved. He bent down, sniffed my skin and whispered…."Get on your knees."

Being hastily obedient, I positioned my body onto my hands and knees. Standing over me, he slowly unzipped my blouse, exposing the bareness of my back. He then lifted my skirt, revealing my naked ass. When the coldness touched my skin, it began to bump with chills.

"Take everything off and resume the same position."

Doing as ordered, I bend back onto my hands and knees and slowly pushed my ass up and lowered my back for more height. I looked back over my shoulder and slung my long locs to the right, where a wisp of hair remained on the nape of my neck.

"Purr if you want it." With my looking perplexed, he continued, "Not the meow-like purr but the deep, throaty purr as if I'm already inside and you are working hard for these dollars that I'm about to rain on you."

With the possibility of BJ moving out, two kids, private school fees, and a mortgage, the thought of earning a few dollars for something that was sheer pleasure to me was both appealing and a turn-on. Dollars began cascading around me and he made it rain again and again, covering me in a blanket of cash. I purred.

The snippets came first, via text, of a partial ass cheek. Similar pictures of my eyes, a breast and my wedding ring, were sent to my home. I was both afraid and perplexed. I had not seen Wright Reynolds sexually, since the night he paid, what totaled, ten thousand dollars for me to purr. After making that investment in me, he wanted to see me again. I did not want an ongoing affair and declined his requests to see me again. After much probing, it *appeared* that BJ was not cheating so I decided to stay with my husband and thought it best to forget the sexpisode with Wright Reynolds ever happened. I wanted to focus on trying to rebuild my life with BJ again.

As I drove to work, I fought against every instinct that suggested Wright was behind this naughty bit of black-text-mailing. BJ and I were finally in a place of building trust and this infidelity would surely be the final ending of so many endings in our marriage. I searched my mind for reasons of the graphic nudes. Who knew enough about me to mail packages to my home that BJ could possibly find? Trying to decide how to approach Wright Reynolds in hopes of sparking up idle chit chat would not be easy. Yet, it had to be done. With all faculty and staff on their way to a professional development workshop, I thought this to be the perfect timing to walk to the gym in hopes of seeing him coaching the basketball team.

I scanned the gym but Wright was not there. I quickly turned back to wave a quick to goodbye to the dancers, while still walking forward. Hands were abruptly placed around my waist to avoid a body to body collision. My face literally inches from the sexiest, best smelling, shortest man ever- whose hands sent shockwaves throughout my entire body. *Be-jesus this mutha is fine.* Quickly becoming conscious that many eyes were looking at us, I broke away from the hold of Wright Reynolds only to turn and face a clearly pissed off looking, caramel-face-colored, tight-skirt-wearing, blonde-weave-sporting, six-inch-heel-strutting, attitude-daring sister.

She was openly sizing up my long-lock-flowing, chocolate-skin-sporting, big-butt-flexing, tiny-waist-showing, confidence-boasting, self.

Yeah, bitch. My eyes quietly challenged. *You should be worried.* Politely acknowledging her, I waited for Wright to introduce us. Apparently, so was she. Exchanging pleasantries through clinched teeth, she spoke coldly.

"I'm Mrs. Reynolds. Wright's wife."

Well, I would hope you're Mrs. Reynolds if you're his wife. I thought. *Dumb bitch.*

I smiled politely. "Nice to meet you, Mrs. Reynolds."

"And you are?"

Wright moved to face her. "She's the school psychologist."

Clearly wanting to slap his ass, she coldly smiled, showing a gap as wide and an ass crack.

"I wasn't talking to you. I was talking to her." This woman was pissed off and wanted me to know it.

"Jade, we ain't even gonna do this shit today. This is my co-worker."

Solidifying her stance, she presses on. "I know that she's your effing co-worker, Wright. What's wrong with me asking for her name? You act like you got something to hide."

"Jade, ain't nobody hiding nothing. You all on this woman for no reason."

Turning towards a voice calling my name, I see Jessie Jameson waving me over and waving to Wright simultaneously.

Glad for the interruption, I excused myself from Wright's obviously, suspecting wife. Jessie placed her arm in mine and forced me to walk with her.

"Girl, ain't nobody got time for that mess. His wife is a trip, honey. I ain't one to gossip, but uuuruhh..." Jessica paused to look at me and we both exploded into loud guffaws and snorts. I took a fast glance back at Wright Reynolds and Jade who was really in his face, pointing fingers, rolling the neck, and eventually, stomping off.

"What is up with those two, Jessie?" I asked.

"Girl, Imma give you the quick rundown."

JessieJames, as she was affectionately known, was a statuesque woman with an old-school, gelled updo and one gold tooth in front. She was a no-nonsense Chicagoan who moved to Atlanta ten years ago after her son was murdered in a drug deal gone bad. Searching for a new start, she secured a job as a School Resource Officer. An absolute joy to be of company, she knew a little bit about everything that was happening in the school. Walking into her office to finish the conversation, I plopped down in a comfy chair and kicked off my shoes.

"I just had to save you from that mess, honey. She used to work here and started messin' with Nugget."

"Nugget?"

"Yes honey. Nugget. He ain't no bigger than a peanut and jes' like a lil' nugget, small and precious. I couldn't call the man Peanut, honey, so I went with Nugget. He's alright with it and even answers to it. But we cool like that. I'm the only one who calls him that. Anyway, she got with him and took him from the teacher here that he was engaged to."

Getting up to get a coke from Jessie's fridge, I took a big gulp before sitting back down. She took a bite of her reheated beans.

"Yes honey. She turned his lil' ass out, whipped up on his fiancé and got fired. But she got her man. Well, if you can call it that. These women up here are crazy over that lil Nugget and I know for sure he's had quite a few of them. Word has it that he's had you too. That's why she all up your Kool-Aid, honey." Cocking her head to the side, Jessie looked for my reaction and waited for a response.

"Well, a rumor is just that. I have not been with Wright Reynolds. I am not saying that he doesn't look good, but I am not a stranger to the school system. I know how shit works, Jessie. People see you talking and automatically think you're fucking em'. Well, I ain't."

I lied. Technically, it wasn't a lie. I never said that I had not experienced it, only that I wasn't now.

"Honey, it's alright. If I thought he'd let me take a dip, I would. And drown his lil short ass in all this." She started rolling her body like a snake from side-to-side and back-to-front. Her antics sent me over the top with more guffaws, snorts, belly-aching, and tearing laughter. Interrupted by a knock on the door, Wright Reynolds entered with a coolness that calmed our laughter.

Not knowing if he heard our conversation, Jessie brazenly uttered, "I was just talking about you, Nugget." She hugged him quickly.

"Well, I hope it was good talk, baby." He looked over at me. "I want to apologize to you on behalf of my wife, Jacobs. She's the jealous type."

"*Umph*. She ain't jealous," Jessie blurted. "She's just crazy as hell. I keep telling folk, how you get em' is how you lose em'. Ain't that right, Nugget?"

Sensing his growing discomfort in knowing that I probably knew their history, I opted to excuse myself, citing work to finish.

"Well, Imma use the bathroom and be right back, Nugget. These damn pinto beans bubbling all through my stomach. Jacobs, I will see you tomorrow."

Not waiting for a response, she left the room and hurried down the hallway with her butt cheeks squeezed together, trying to make it to the bathroom without an unpleasant incident.

The heat between us was smoldering. I wanted him right there, right now. I found it hard to breathe with him so close to me. I attempted to move aside but he blocked me. Standing close enough to whisper in my ear, he sniffed my skin, nibbled my earlobe, and placed my hand on his pants to feel his hardness. I kept it there. He moaned and I became lost in his sounds. Moving his hand down to the small of my back, my brain told my body to move away and my body responded, *"Fuck you."* The excitement of knowing that we were having a naughty bit in someone else's office was mind-altering. It was altered all the way down to stupid status. He kissed me. I kissed him back.

Really, have you not learned anything from Craig? Are you really getting it on in the RESOURCE OFFICER's OFFICE! I moaned out loud. *"Shut the fuck up mind!"* Not hearing the door open but feeling nails dig into my face, Jade was upon me. I immediately began to defend myself by throwing punches and adding a few kicks of my own. Trying to get between us but mostly grabbing her, Wright Reynolds received more than his fair share of punches, kicks, and scratches as Jade released her wrath.

JessieJames rushed in and used her large frame to shield me from the stiletto that Jade was swinging and it struck her instead. One swing of the back of Jessie's strong hand sent Jade falling swiftly into a corner, knocking the wind out of her.

"Not on my watch baby girl," she said. "You done ran up on the wrong one now. You gotta take this ghetto shit back to the hood, honey." Pushing Wright to the side, Jessie aggressively pulled Jade to her feet, cuffed her to the arrest bar, and then called the police and principal.

Thankfully, most of the staff and faculty had already gone home for the day. But I knew that it would only be a matter of time before it was the talk of the school.

"Bitch, I knew you was fucking him still! Y'all walking around here acting like y'all barely know each other."

Jade began to sob uncontrollably and Wright moved to console her. She spat in in face.

"Don't you fucking touch me, wicho' black cheating ass! Don't you fucking touch me! This shit ain't right! It ain't right! I'm about to go to jail over some bullshit bitch! All 'cause you can't keep your dick in your pants! You told me we were good but I knew you were lying. I knew it and gave you a chance to come clean so many fucking times. I should've fucking left your ass when I said I would." Then she directed her anger toward Jessie.

"Why *she* ain't got no goddamn handcuffs on, huh?"

"Because," JessieJames said. "You attacked her and me with a weapon."

"I ain't got no fucking weapon! I was just swinging on her ass with my shoe!"

"Exactly!"

Not believing what just happened, I stood in the corner of the room, dazed. My face was scratched and bleeding, my lip busted, and stomach hurting.

"Wait. Is that one, no two, of my locs on the floor?

"Do you need an *ammalance,* honey?" Jessie asked. "If not, I got some alcohol to put on them scratches to take any infection out before it set in good, 'cause her nails look dirty."

Not wanting to laugh at Jessie, but not being able to stop myself, I began to snicker at her joke.

"Jacobs, honey, you know you might lose your job, right? You sat right before me and lied. You know you saw Nugget outside of work and as soon as he walked in, I seen it. What I didn't know that is she seen it too. You know, probably won't nothing happen to Nugget 'cause he didn't do nothing. Well, he kinda' did. Honey, I don't know what's gone happen. I'm just thinking what might happen."

I replayed Jade's words, she said "still." She said, 'Fucking him *still.*' The police arrived to take Jade away and I prepared for my probable termination. Jade, that all-the-while-knowing, stiletto-swinging cussing, angry-wife-revenging-hater, got the last word on this honest-face-lying, lusting-wife-cheating, purring-kitty-kat-earning, liar.

She turned to me and stared directly into my eyes.

"That was my apartment that you were purring in. Wright secretly made a video of you two and I found it.

I sent those texts to your phone and mailed the pictures to your house, you nasty bitch. That was my ten thousand dollars that he rained on your big funky black ass. I know your type because I used to be just like you. I know BJ personally. That's how I knew where you lived. It's decorated nicely." She twisted her mouth into a sinister grin.

"And that IM came from me. I've been holding BJ down for a while now but never knew who his wife was until I saw y'all at the Velvet Room. I also saw Wright talking to you. It's just a coincidence that you were fucking my husband, while I was fucking yours.

Oh by the way, I sent him the video too."

Write, share, and discuss with others your thoughts about this short story. What do you think happens next? What emotions surface as you read this story? Explain why you feel this way.

The Something (A Bit)

He raped me and I convinced myself that it was okay. He told me that he had been watching me through my living room window and knew then that he had to have me. I smiled a sick flattery towards a man that I had always secretly wanted, but was afraid to have. I was too frightened to say no, because I knew that rejecting him would not matter but would only make the act more brutal and forceful.

He was inside of my home, preparing to invade me and it both excited and frightened me. I was forever intrigued from afar, but knew that aggression was his way of life, so I always stayed away.

At first, I struggled for release but soon felt the pressure of being overpowered and surrendered. I convinced myself that surrendering was the right thing to do. After all, I was the one who had allowed him into my home. People would blame me before they believed me so I embraced the movements but not the man.

It happened quickly. Knowing his history of violent behavior, I relaxed against him with each engagement while he continued to rip more of my silk red gown away from my now shamelessly willing body, yet recoiling mind. He clutched and lifted my ass tightly for leverage while forcing my body to move with his.

As he moved inside me over-and-over again, his semen escaped into me like poison running through my veins. He refused to turn off the lights and stared directly into my eyes, which met his and never lost connection. Within those eyes, I saw an ominous fury of conquest and conqueror, strength and weakness, aggression and submission, love and hate, and when it was over, pain and apology.

I could tell that he was satisfactorily stimulated as he pulled from inside me. He drew his pants from his knees and said, "I'll call you tomorrow. You are now mine." I was repulsed yet felt that I indeed belonged to him, but only in the worst way. After he left, my mind was ashamed. My skin crawled of invisible dirt. My abused body betrayed me and overruled repulsion with a wetness and longing for more of his forcefulness venom.

I told no one.

He called often and used his middle name when he left messages for me. I would never call back.

"Who is this Adam person that continues to call you?" Mom asked.

"A friend from school", I lied. "Do you remember the guy that I dated from school that you didn't like?"

"Yes," she said. "I remember him, but his name was not Adam."

I lied once more. "Adam is his middle name."

She rolled her eyes and walked off.

"No wonder he is so quick to hang up," she said.

I felt a sigh of relief, convinced that this conversation would not present itself again.

I had no desire to talk to him, yet found myself having a desire to feel him again. I was uncomfortable and questioned whether or not I had really been raped or just a willing sexual victim. A victim was not supposed to be willing or intrigued when her attacker rang. The nauseous component was that he truly did not think that he had done anything wrong. He began to claim me as his and I secretly accepted.

He called again and Mom answered. She rolled her eyes and passed me the phone. "I can't stand him and I wish he would stop calling my house."

My mind flooded with a thousand questions as I felt his fury through the phone. I became both afraid and glad that I was home and not in his presence.

"I've driven by your house every night and know that you are there, yet you do not answer your phone, forcing me to call your house. Why are you doing this?"

Before I could answer, he continued.

"Do you not want to be in this relationship with me anymore?"

Relationship? I thought. His voice softened.

"I want to take you to dinner and a movie. I admit that we should not have started our relationship off making love, but I was so excited to be in your space and thought if this was the only chance I would ever have to feel you, then I must the seize moment."

Doubt challenged my assuredness. I contemplated the possibility of passion.

He said that we made love. "Did we?" I asked myself aloud. *Am I the one who is confused? Did I somehow lead him to this? He's speaking to me as if...as if...as if we* really *made love.*

"Did we what?" He asked, breaking my thoughts.

"Are you going to answer me? Will you meet me, tonight?"

Silence.

"We can just sit and talk if you do not want dinner and a movie."

More silence and one heartbeat.

"I know you're not sure. I promise that I will not touch you this time".

Silence again and two heartbeats.

"I'll come by your house and blow the horn. Just come out. I can't wait to see you." He hung up.

Before placing the phone on the receiver, I held it a little longer to my ear.

"I can't wait to see you, too."

Write, share, and discuss with others your thoughts about this intense story. What do you think happens next? What emotions surface as you read this short? Should she question her actions? Explain why you feel this way.

The Other Side of 10 Days

The sun don't shine that much on this side of town. Lying on the cold, wet pavement with my face pressed hard against it, I could taste the blood slowly oozing from my split tongue. I contemplated that this was what going to hell felt like. Thoughts drifted to the unfulfilled promise that something better was out there that I had yet to discover. I wondered if this was the life that God had planned for me.

Someone once said, "Whenever your experience doesn't line up with your expectations, God is trying to give you a revelation." My momma would call it embarrassment by eradication but 10 days ago, none of this mattered.

Now feeling the pressure of a 357 on the back of my head, I wondered if this was the day that Momma had been promising would come to me while showing me the dress that she would wear to my funeral. Hearing laughter around me as a foot grinded the feces further into my already heavily-soiled underwear, I began to pray and brace myself for the shot that was sure to come, to the back of my head.

Just days ago, I was sitting at the kitchen table, having a conversation with Momma. Watching her shuffle through the kitchen to fix me a hot plate, I wondered why, even with all of the unkind pleasures that the ghetto had shown her, she still showed me only love.

"Where you going tonight, Sam?" She asked. "I am still getting hang-up phone calls from someone that I know is looking for you. You gone go and git yo'self killed and leave me here all by myself. I ain't got no money to bury you wit, so you'll go in a pine box, I suppose. It's up to you to decide if it's gonna be hell or heaven. You already living in hell here on earth. I don't see why you wanna make hell yo' eternal promise. Yo' daddy died in violence but that wasn't none of his fault and now you gone run to yo' death? You ready to leave this earth that bad? What about your son? Don't you think he needs you?"

Momma questioned with hurt and frustration as she always did. Getting up to give her a hug, but never answering her questions, I tried to reassure her.

"Momma, your baby boy's gon' be jes' fine."

Squeezing my hand, she said that she did not want to be late for church because she needed to ask the church to pray for me. She left strict instructions for me to wash my plate after I finished eating. With that, she disappeared out the door.

Even though I said that all was well, anyone who knew me knew that I was in a whole lot of trouble. I was safe as long as I was in Momma's house, as there was an unspoken rule on the streets to never hurt the mommas after a major gang member's momma was killed in the midst of a shootout at her home. But what was I to do? I had to leave. I had to make that cheese to repay what I owed to the streets. There would be no tomorrow for me, if I didn't. I'd been hiding out for a few months at different places trying to figure out how I was gonna replace the money for the crack that I had smoked up from a dealer in a neighboring city.

Fooling myself that I could outrun the pull of the pipe, I convinced Vince to let me hold down the corner to make some money to support my newborn son, Elijah. Just two days into his new life, six years ago, I decided to celebrate by trying the pipe. I have not seen my son much since. The poison fruit paralyzed my mind and compromised my soul in one hit. Just as quickly as it came, the high was gone. I had a whole stash of shit and told myself that I could pay it back. I couldn't and left town.

Now I found myself doing the same thing and smokin' up a dealers crack. I had been off the block for hours with no product and no money for Vince. Scared to return empty handed, I convinced a long term crackhead to hit me with a bottle in the back of the head.

I dragged my bleeding body back to the corner, lying that someone had robbed me. Vince put the word out that dollars would be paid for turning in the person who stole his shit. To protect myself from being told on, I casually mentioned to Steel, the watcher, the name of the crackhead who hit me. He was dead within minutes.

I quickly earned the reputation as being soft because a crackhead had robbed me and took my stash. I could live with that reputation because it allowed me to use that as an excuse a couple more times and keep using without being suspected. I knew something had changed when I was taken off the corner.

Sitting in front of Vince, there was an unknown familiarity with him that I could not resolve. I was shaking from the sheer fear of him and my need for another fix. Surrounded by Steel and several other gun-carrying gang members, I tried to convince Vince that I was clean.

"You hittin' that pipe?" Vince asked.

"Naw man. You know me." I said.

"I do know your monkey ass and I know that you been stealing my shit and owe me money! About ten muthafuckin' grand, crack head!"

"Yo, I ain't no crack head, man, and I ain't stole yo' shit. I-I told you that s-somebody robbed me man."

"Nigga, I will blow your head off right now if you say dat' shit again, you heard? So dis here what's gone go down. 'Cuz you used to be my nigga, Imma give you 10 days to get my 10 grand back in my hand before I get at cha'. I'm only doin dat' cuz I like yo' momma. She was real good to us when we was little, after my momma died. Yo' momma fed me for 10 days, gave me a place to lay my head, and washed my clothes when my own Momma died of an overdose. Not only dat', she made sho' she stayed wit' us until other family came to claim me so I wouldn't go to tha' state.

"So, because of yo' Momma, Imma give you 10 days, too. But since you say you clean, Imma give you this bag, if you suck Steel's dick."

I suddenly remembered my conversation with Momma.

"What's wrong with you, Sam? Why you been gone for days? Why you ain't eatin'? Why folks come telling me that you in dem crack houses and doing drugs?"

"Momma I ain't doing nothing," I lied. "I been spending time with Elijah. That's why I ain't been home." More lies. Momma paced slowly across the room praying for my spirit and soul to be saved.

"Sam, you can't deal with the sickness of your body until you deal wit' the separation of yo' spirit. Yo' spirit is dead, son."

"So what's it gonna be, my nigga?" Vince asked, snapping me back into reality. "You want this hit bad enough to suck it?"

"Man, nooooo! I told you I ain't no crack head and I ain't gone do no crackhead shit! Imma get cho' money man. Imma get cho money".

Vince motioned for Steel to open the door and lead me out. As Steel walked in front of me, for the first time I noticed how tight and muscular his arms were and how thick and strong his thighs appeared to be. Standing over six feet tall, Steel had been shot atleast four times and honestly earned the title of his nickname. His strong, silent presence and cold stare of disgust let me know that he would shoot me in the head before letting me put my lips around any part of his body. My body wanted that crack so strongly, that had I been urged much longer, I surely would have sucked him off. Momma was right, my spirit was dead.

Day 1

I forced my mind to convince my body that it no longer needed to feed from crack and needed a place to fight this demon. There were not many places that a crackhead could hide, as abandoned buildings were like food stamps to us—free and spread quickly.

God was watching over me during this time and sent Momma on an extended seniors cruise and tour with the church full of gospel music, activities, and preaching.

I stood watching and waiting around the corner, praying that she'd hurry and board the bus so that I could go home. I spoke with Momma earlier that day to let her know that her baby boy was alright and loved himself his Momma. Laughing some comfort into my spirit, Momma told me that she had prepared enough food for me until she gets back and that I should clean up after myself. *That's my Momma.*

Day 5

My body rebelled with painfully strong convulsions of vomiting and dry heaving, while constantly negotiating with my brain for just one more hit. My mind fought harder, pounding my body with images of Momma and Elijah. Saturated with sweat, I tore my clothes away because I was hot and my clothes were wet and sticky. Then I searched frantically for them because I was cold and naked. My mind played cruel tricks and showed me happy visions of lighting the pipe and relaxing into its essence.

More than once, I attempted to make my way out the door but was too weak to stand. I thought that if I could just get enough strength to stand, I would sell Momma's most valuable items to pay back Vince or buy a few hits. I knew that she would forgive me even if she never spoke to me again. Her belongings would only get me enough money to buy a few hits because the streets know what you want the money for and how desperate you are to get it, so they hustle you down to a hit and a promise of another hit if you can score some more shit to boost. I slept for four days.

Day 9

The front door opened. I heard Momma moving from room-to-room checking to see if the house was intact and clean. The refrigerator door opened and Momma began to speak with herself.

"Lord, that boy ain't ate nothing. Good thing I froze them dinners or all my good food would've went to waste." I heard her say while heading to my room. The phone rang, switching Momma's direction. I was thankful, as it gave me a chance to try and air the room and clean up the vomit from the floor.

Nine days had come and almost gone and I didn't remember much from them. My body felt empty and angry.

"Imma drug addict." I spoke these words to myself over-and-over, while slowly pulling myself upright.

I overheard Momma talking about the trip with her church friend while heating up some food. She complained that the dinners that she'd cooked before leaving would've spoiled had she not frozen them. She was happy and spoke of the great music and fun activities and great preaching, while making her way towards her room.

Thankful for the moment, I quickly moved into the kitchen and grabbed a cloth to wet and wipe up the vomit. I changed the sheets on my single bed and stuffed the old ones underneath the bed. I opened the window slightly to let the stale city air inside.

Passing by the broken mirror, I caught a glimpse of myself. I looked as if I was just coming off a drinking binge. My body was noticeably thinner.

Imma drug addict, I thought again. Slipping down the hallway into the bathroom, I managed to wash my face and change clothes before pretending to just get home. I opened and closed the front door and yelled, "Momma!"

Emerging from her room and still on the phone, she waved quickly, held up the "one more minute" index finger and pointed for me to check the heating food.

I took the food out the oven and set plates. Momma had a million stories about the preaching, food, and over-the-top clothes and hats. She was a great follower of Bishop T.D. Jakes, so he was the highlight of her trip. Thankful that the trip had overshadowed any questions about me, the phone rang again soon after we sat down for dinner and Momma was off to tell yet another story about the preaching. I quietly slid into the shower and back into my bed. I was grateful to hear the familiarity of Momma moving about the house, humming and praying. For the first time in days, I fell into a peaceful sleep while my spirit began its journey of healing.

10 Days

I knew there was no way of paying Vince back and spent my day with Momma catching up, laughing and bonding. I made up stories about Elijah so that she would think that I spent my days and nights with him while she was gone, which accounted for my not eating the cooked meals that we were now eating. Reminding me to clean up afterwards, Momma squeezed my shoulders and left for church. My ten days were up I was scared that I was going to die but refused to hide any longer. I walked out the door and I asked God to save my life and my soul.

I defecated in my pants the moment that I saw Steel turn the corner. Steel threw me to the ground and my face hit the pavement, splitting my tongue and spewing blood. Vince stood on top of my backside and put one foot on my ass, pressing the shit further into my body- while the other foot was on my face, grinding it deeper into the cement. He then bent over and placed the barrel of a gun to the back of my head. I closed my eyes preparing to die.

"Kill your brother, Vince, and you may as well kill me, too!" A familiar voice cried out. "Yo' daddy would've been so disappointed in the way that you living your life. He died because some drug addict robbed and stabbed him on the street, leaving him for dead and now you gone kill your own brother? God got better plans for your life, son."

Brother? My mind raced.

"I ain't cho' damn son! Jes cause you fed me and kept me for 10 days after my Momma died don't make me yo' son! Yo' boy and you say, my *brother*, stole my drugs and my money. I want it back. And if he can't pay by money, he gone pay with his life."

The familiarity that I could not place was now resolved. Vince was my father's son. His face resembled our Father. Strong cheek bones, stern, cold stare, and chilling laughter.

"I ain't gone stand by and let you kill my son, Vince, and not say nothing to nobody.

No, Momma, I thought.

"I'm an old woman and I only fear God himself. If yo' brother stole from you, then you should forgive him. Not kill him." Momma preached and then began to pray the words,

"May God forgive your broken soul." Vince cocked the gun.

"Noooooooo!" I screamed.

There were two shots fired. The first shot was for Momma and the second shot was for me. That day, we both died.

Write, share, and discuss with others your thoughts about this story. What emotions surface as you read this short? Explain why you feel this way.

The Exchange (A Bit)

"It was only a bad dream," she kept repeating while cradling me tightly. "It was only a bad dream."

I clearly remembered, ten years ago, the awful night that she allowed someone to take me for a ten-rock high. It was not a bad dream but maybe she needed for it to be so that she did not have to deal with the reality of shaping my now shattered life of promiscuity, drugs, and disease.

It was the morning of my birthday and the sun was breaking through darkness to dawn. Although I had never experienced a real birthday party, Mama and I always shared a cupcake for each year of my existence. Today, there were no cupcakes and Mama, like the streets below, had been moving restlessly throughout the night unable able to sit, stand, or sleep.

I had seen those symptoms too many times before and no amount of hugs, kisses, or sweet storytelling was going to get her through this. She needed a fix. She sipped on cheap gin to help curb the pains from being drug dry, but her body quickly became immune. She needed the kind of poison that set her insides on fire and cooled her skin. The kind of poison that partnered her desire with the willpower that was supposed to help her to overcome.

Her body reeked and her hair was matted from lack of combing and washing. As she rocked back-and-forth with sobs from the aches and pains, I found myself mimicking her anguish with the same movements she was projecting.

As I moved to comfort her sullen state, he appeared. Without notice, permission, or invitation, he simply appeared. With shiny teeth of gold and a face full of oil and pimples, he stood in front of her as she reached to unzip his pants.

In the past, I had always been instructed to hide before company arrived, but this time I watched and waited to see what her silent words meant. Her eyes pleaded apologies and motioned for me to leave. He noticed and traced her eyes back to me. That vile, oily-faced man quickly moved away from her and pointed at me.

"Four rocks for her."

"No!" Mama screamed.

"Six, then."

Again, mom refused, but with hesitation. As I began to back away, I knew that whatever those numbers meant, it was not good for me. Then she said two words that would change my life forever.

"Ten rocks."

He agreed.

The deal was made and the product was exchanged. I was, without delay, snatched up as she disappeared into the bathroom, closing the door to my innocence, my future, my life.

Happy birthday.

Write, share, and discuss with others your thoughts about this powerful bit. What do you think happens next? Explain why you feel this way.

Sharing with Division

I dropped off my last load in Virginia and pulled into the Lazy Beaver Rest Stop to get a quick bite and sleep before making the 12-hour drive back home. The hookers moved swiftly from rig-to-rig trying to make a fast dollar turning tricks and I wondered what their lives consisted of outside the hustle. As I watched them dart between the trucks, a scantily-clad lady approached. With my rig still running, she stepped onto my board and smiled, displaying a set of rotted brown-colored teeth. With the truck window unwound, I saw that she looked tired and aged. Her skin was full with pimples that had scalped into crater-like holes.

Through thin lips crusted and scarred, she asked, "You want some company, honey?" I shook my head no and turned away. Now tapping on the window, she continued. "I just want to get out of the cold. Can I please at least sit in some warmth? I will make it worth your while."

I wanted to respond, "I don't do women," but that would have been a lie, so I reached into my console and pulled out a twenty-dollar bill. She immediately became excited at the sight of it and began to lick her thin lips.

"This is what you really want, right?"

She shook her head feverishly as I cracked the window quickly sliding the money through, it fell. I watched her chase the twenty-dollar bill against the blowing wind. As she bent over to pick up the bill, she exposed torn red panties that barely covered her skinny thighs and boney hips. She snatched up the money and ran to a waiting car. She disappeared into the night as quickly as she appeared, leaving me alone to think about my life.

When I was younger, my Momma used to always say, “You ain’t the most beautiful thing, but you should be able to find somebody who might want a fat, black gal wit’ nappy hair. If you ain’t got no money to take care of dem’, you got to give them the juicy between yo thighs to keep em’. So, dey want you.”

My Momma never made me feel beautiful. Being an exact image of her, she took pleasure in projecting the hurt unto me that many men had unto her. Weighing almost four-hundred pounds and still gaining, my Momma’s sheer appearance forced me want to work hard to be my own success and not live in her shadow, or within the shadows, of the parade of married men who constantly used her juicy for their own nasty pleasures. My Momma was a broken woman and accepted her eat-piss-shit-and-sleep life as is. I wanted more.

As an only child, I enjoyed working on big trucks at the garage with my daddy. He didn’t have much book smarts but he taught me the only skills he knew which were how to repair trucks and save money. I barely graduated from high school and clearly was not of collegiate material, so I decided to become a hauler. I eventually saved enough money to start my own trucking company. After two years in business, I purchased a second rig. Being a small business owner, I was forced to drive one of my own trucks. The numerous small contracts continued to grow my business, keeping me away from home and away from Armon.

I met Armon on a social networking site for small business owners and found him intriguing. A mortgage broker who lived in Georgia, Armon had successfully kept his business thriving, where many others failed during the crash. Armon and I skyped often and he eventually invited me to visit him. After a few sexually charged stopovers, I relocated to Atlanta and into Armon's home.

Atlanta was definitely a single person's city that was full of night clubs, strip clubs, and plenty of beautiful single women. Tall, biracial, and well-defined with green eyes, Armon was attractive enough to have his choice of any woman. I was in stark contrast to what the world considered beautiful. With my dark skin and common face, I constantly lived in a state of insecurity and would often ask Armon, "Why are you still single?"

He would always respond, "I'm not single, because I have you, Kita."

Inside, my heart buzzed and I felt that I had hit the jackpot.

"You sure do have me, baby. You sure do."

In my deepest thoughts, I was feeling very satisfied with not living the whorish lifestyle that Momma had claimed for me. I had my own business, a beautiful yellow man, and someone who did not use me for my juicy.

My body starting to heat up thinking about Armon. I decided to put the pedal to the metal and make the drive home that night. "Some of that super-sized manhood would definitely hit the spot right now," I said aloud to myself. "So, I'm going to surprise him and head home."

The long drive home continued to seduce my thoughts as I replayed my life with Armon. Things had not always been easy with him in the beginning. Moving into his lifestyle often gave me pause and left me wondering if I had left one bad relationship to endure the same shit, only with a different man.

Armon had lots of female friends who would just show up and sometimes stay over. It was a difficult transition for me but he assured me that they were just longtime friends whom he opened his doors to from time-to-time. My instincts advised me differently and begged me to leave while my heart still belonged to me. But who was I kidding? Armon was the best chance that I would ever get in a relationship and he already owned my heart.

I recalled the first time that I met her.

Armon and I had only been living together for six months and I had just returned home after a long stretch on the road. I was excited about seeing Armon and did not tell him that I was on my way. I opened the door to find him sitting closely with another woman on my sofa.

"What the fuck is going on here!" I yelled.

"This is my girl, Kita." Armon answered calmly.

I closely examined the girl and continued talking to him. "Your 'girl'?" I paced back and forth, breathing heavily and refusing to sit down. "What the fuck, Armon?"

I moved toward the pretty woman sitting on my expensive sofa, "I'm about to get at you and get at this bitch!" She didn't flinch, as Armon stood to place his tall frame between the pretty woman and myself.

"No, you are not, Kita. What did you think was going to happen with your being on the road all the time and leaving me here alone?"

"I expected your ass to be faithful." I said coldly. "You coulda' least told me that you needed me home more to see what I could do before you go sexing somebody else. How long this been going on?"

I began to recall the little signs like the half-used bottle of apricot body wash in the shower that he said he was using. And the new satin sheets on the bed that he said he bought for us.

"All lies," I blurted. "She's been in my house all the times that I have not."

"This ain't cho' house, Kita," Armon laughed. "This is *my* house."

I rushed to the kitchen, picked up the unpaid bills, and began throwing them at him.

"You see this fucking water bill, light bill, car note, and rent receipt, Armon? I've been paying the bills in this expensive-ass apartment while you and your bitch have been chillin' off me, but this ain't my house? This ain't my house! I ain't believing this shit!"

In my disbelief, it became hard to breathe. I walked outside for some fresh air and to regroup. Armon followed.

"It ain't gotta be like this, Kita. I didn't mean to hurt you, baby. You know I love you. I just want you to consider tryna make this lil' triangle work for all of us."

Did he just ask me, in his own way, if he could keep her?

"I will not allow this, Armon. I will not be second in my home. Excuse me—*your* home."

"You won't be second, baby. You still my main squeeze, but you kinda' knew the deal when you moved in."

"There was no deal, Armon. You invited me into your home as your woman. You never said that I would be sharing you with someone else." Armon attempted to hold me as I pushed him away. My tears began to quietly flow.

"I didn't expect for you to be faithful to me forever. Hell, what man is?" I sighed. "But I sure as hell didn't expect for you to introduce me to your other girlfriend like I would be cool with that. I know that I don't look like that lil' light-skinned bitch you got in there, but I also know my own self-worth. You chose *me*! You came for *me*! You get that lil' trick to pay your bills now that your money is short and your business done fell off and see how long she lasts." I shoved Armon and turned to leave, but he grabbed my arm.

"Move outta my way, Armon, I don't get down like that no mo'. Imma come get my shit tomorrow so make sure your skinny-light-skinned, fake-hair-wearing bitch ain't here." I continued, yelling over my shoulder. "Or Imma break that skinny, toothpick-ass-looking bitch in two!"

"Her name is Giselle, Kita. Not 'skinny little bitch.'"

As I stormed past the neighbors who had gathered outside, I could hear one woman say to another, "Girl, she just don't know. Armon been having relationships with them damn strippers for years and he sho' ain't gon' stop cuz she paying his rent."

The other woman replied, "Girl, you know she gotta be making some money 'cause Armon wouldn't be wit' nobody like her just because."

A third spectator chimed in. "Ain't she big, though? She don't look nuthin' like his other women. She sho' must have a lotta money for him to lay with that." Nodding to himself, "He da' man up- in- here. Sho' you right."

With both my feelings and ego damaged, I climbed into my rig and drove to a hotel to gather my thoughts and plan my next move. As Armon rang my phone all night, I finally turned it off to find sleep but only awakened with tears streaming from my eyes. My heart was broken. I sat up and replayed the scene at Armon's and realized that I really loved him, despite his infidelities. I simply did not want to experience yet another epic relationship failure.

I am on the road often, I rationalized. Perhaps I was being naïve to hope that he should, not necessarily would, be faithful with my being gone for such long stretches. She was beautiful, that yellow girl. She was more Armon's type than me. She was everything that I was not with her flawless high-yellow skin, small waist, long legs and perfectly manicured toes. She represented everything that I wanted to physically see in myself as a woman.

With my Momma's words resonating throughout my mind, I suddenly felt ugly in my dark skin, nappy hair, and burdensome burly body. Giselle was the epitome of femininity and confidence and I lived in a body of masculinity and self-hatred.

I could never compare nor compete with neither her beauty nor Armon's desire for her. Clearly, Armon must love me still, I guessed, because he asked for my understanding and acceptance. He didn't want me to leave just to accept that he wanted her to stay. It would not be so bad, maybe, if he promised that she would never be around us. I allowed myself to believe that I was better off with Armon than without him, accommodating my own decision of sharing with division.

Write, share, and discuss with others your thoughts about this story. Would you share? What emotions surface as you read this short story? Explain why you feel this way.

SLIPPIN'

Bright and early on a Monday Morning, Timothy Serry is preparing for his morning radio show.

"Good morning Chicago. All is well in the windy city and you are rolling with the Ser-Tim and the Family morning show. The question of the day is: Can a traveling woman hold a good man down?"

"My wife Lea, has been gone for two weeks now, chasing that almighty paper when she should be at home trying to hold a brotha down, right? I am going to get Lea on the phone, so that she can either be down or get broken down. What's up, Atlanta? Holla at cha' boy!"

Lea Serry and Timothy Serry - The Meeting

Lea Serry, a hard-nosed defense attorney, always dreamed of becoming the female version of Johnny Cochran. Graduating at the top of her class from Harvard University, she was sought after by top law firms across the nation.

Inking a six-figure deal with a top law firm in Connecticut after graduation, Lea flew back to Atlanta to celebrate with her Nana Aims who raised her when her Mom was incarcerated. Lea took a quiet moment to sit and reflect on how difficult it was growing up as a child and how thankful she was that God had blessed her with a loving and committed grandmother, whom she vowed to always care for.

Noticing an unfamiliar face laughing heartily with her cousin Avery, Lea walked over to say hello.

"Hey, cuz," said Avery. "Congrats on that new job. We got a big-time lawyer in da' hiz-ouse!" A scholar himself, Avery was in his third year of medical school with the goal of becoming a heart surgeon.

"I'm not the only brainiac in this family, Avery. You must know that I am proud of you as well and am definitely in your corner."

"I know Lea-Lea. A brother sho' thank ya."

Clearing his throat, Timothy Serry brought attention to himself.

"Oh my bad, man," Avery apologized. "Lea, this is my good friend, Timothy Serry. He and I were roommates at Morehouse."

"The pleasure is all mine. Are you in medical school as well?"

"No," Timothy answered. "I am a DJ at a local radio station here."

Shaking his head, Avery interjected. "Man, stop downplaying. He is *the* DJ to watch, Lea. This is SerTim."

Lea smiled. "I feel privileged, indeed, to be standing in the midst of a local celebrity. I am honored."

After spending the last several years dating only prominent white men who did not necessarily please her sexually, Lea felt an attraction to the modest undertones of this African American man. She had forgotten what it was like to be in the presence of a strong and beautiful black man. Deciding that she wanted to experience him, eleven months and many orgasms later, Lea became Mrs. Timothy Serry.

Lea and Timothy Serry - The Marriage

The marriage was initially exciting, fulfilling, and honest. But after four years of mostly living alone, Tim was now becoming increasingly frustrated with Lea being away from home so often. Living in Connecticut during the weekdays to be closer to the firm, the arrangement worked well the first couple of years until Tim decided that her now seven figure salary did not replace the warmth of her beautiful body. He also wanted desperately to start a family. Lea flew home every weekend to *play* wife, providing that she did not have a big case. She had already missed the last two weekends and looked like a missed third weekend was underway.

A couple months back when visiting home, Lea walked into the bedroom to find Timothy looking through her luggage.

"What are you doing?" she asked.

"I am trying to make sure there are not any birth control pills in this bag, Lea. I am ready to start the family that you promised. I am tired of spending my days and nights without you," said a frustrated Tim. "I want you home and I want a baby for us."

"Am I supposed to just leave my career and salary to play Mommy, Tim?"

"Lea! I don't care about your money or your damn career. I just want to have a family! Don't you understand?"

"Tim, I understand, but do you think that we can live like this on your salary?" Regretting that she said those words, even as she spoke them, Lea saw the hurt on his face and dropped her head.

"Look, Tim." She pulled him close to her. "Baby, I know that you want a family and I promise that you won't find any birth control pills in my bags. I am not taking them any longer, as I promised."

Softly speaking while kissing his lips, she continued.

"My career is very important to me just as yours is important to you, Tim. I have worked hard to solidify my place with this firm. However, you are more important." She unbuttoned his shirt. "I will say this, Tim. I am not planning to have a baby right now, but I am also not planning against it. So, can you just relax, baby, and enjoy our time together?"

Lea intended to wait at least another four years before starting a family, since her goal was to become the youngest and first African American woman to partner with the firm. She had a strong track record and not lost a case since her first trial. She had no intentions of losing any now. She secretly kept another pack of birth control pills at her apartment in Connecticut and would once again resume taking them as soon as she returned home. In the meantime, it was an excellent weekend for making love and she was sure that the double dosage she took before her flight would keep her protected.

Lea was both proud and ashamed for being able to convince Tim that she was trying to have his child then quickly replaced her thoughts of betrayal with thoughts of intimacy. Lea and Tim enjoyed a night filled with many glasses of wine, easy conversations of having children, and passionate love making.

Not feeling well for several weeks now, Lea finally took time from her busy schedule to visit her

Gynecologist as she was past due for a pap smear and thought that might be the reason for her discomfort.

"You're kidding, right? This cannot be true. Pregnant?! How can that be?"

"How do you think?" Responded Dr. Phipps. "Congratulations."

Clearly upset, Lea explained.

"But I was taking my birth control pills a-and…and I never missed a day! I swear!" Dr. Phipps passed her a pamphlet about pregnancy.

"Birth control pills are not a fool proof guarantee, Lea. Only a high percentage safeguard against pregnancy. Are you having second thoughts about the pregnancy?"

"I'm not sure."

Lea left the office in disbelief. She envisioned the partnership disappearing from her grasp, as no one would want to make her a partner if she had baggage. Lea went home to rest and think about her plight.

Forcing herself to awaken to heavy rain at 5:00am the next morning, Lea now regretted not catching the Redeye with the partners to meet with a major client. Instead, she opted to drive the four hours to their 10:00am meeting. She needed to think and simply did not want to share her mental space with the other legal minds. She had a much bigger decision to consider.

Lea had not determined when or if she would tell Tim, as she was still trying to wrap her mind around being with child. She was both anxious and angry and was not ready to change diapers, breastfeed or get fat. She thought about the impending stretch marks, the numerous doctor visits, the interruption of sleep, and rolled her eyes. She was too selfish to give up her freedom, her career, or share her husband.

Lost in her thoughts of selfishness, Lea's cell phone rang. It was Timothy.

"Good morning, babe," Tim greeted. She clicked her car's speaker phone. Feeling annoyed, Lea really did not want to speak with Tim but knew had she not answered, he would have been concerned and continued to call.

"Hey you. I am on the highway driving to a 10:00am. I wish that I'd taken the Red Eye with the partners, but I just wanted to spend some time alone preparing. I miss you, Babe—"

"Ahh, she lying, SerTim," DJ A1 interrupted. The radio staff exploded with laughter.

"I'm on the radio, Tim?"

"You sho' is Lea-baby." A1 said. "What's going, shuga?"

Thankful to hear the sound of laughter and light conversation, Lea relaxed and participated in yet another on the air call, as she often did.

"Thanks guys for the call. I need the company. The roads are wet with light of traffic this time of morning. Conversation is good for me now—."

"Hey Lea," A1 interrupted again. "We're talking about the secret to how women, like you, who stay on the road all the damn time, still manage to take care of home. What's up wit' dat, shuga?"

"Well, what I say is this—"

Suddenly, there was a scream, tires screeching, a crash, and silence. Knowing this was not a joke, but wishing that it was, Tim could hear the sounds of Lea as she gasped for air. No longer caring that thousands of listeners were part of this moment, trying his best to remain composed, Tim slowly began to speak.

"Lea, are you ok, baby?" There was no response. His voice began to tremble. "Lea-baby, what is going on? This is no time for joking." Realizing that this clearly was not a joke but not knowing what else to say, he continued on. "Lea!" He called more urgently. "Lea please, what is going on?"

A raspy voice whispered. "Tim, please help me. I am hurt."

Relieved, Tim cried. "Lea. Where are you, baby?"

"Please help me," she whispered more quietly now. "It's so hard to breathe, Tim."

Tim released his emotions and began to sob. "Lea, I am tracking your GPS, baby." "Help is on the way."

Now desperately wanting to save their unborn child, Lea begged. "Please, Tim. I don't want to die. I don't want our baby to die. Save our baby—please! Please, oh God, please. I do want this baby. Please let me live," she pleaded with God. "My husband…my baby."

Tim could only replay Lea's words of her pregnancy. "My God," he mouthed to A1. "She's *pregnant*?" Feeling helpless and lost in agony, Timothy Serry stood to his feet and unabashedly bawled and could not, for the moment, be consoled. The phones lines began to light up but no one answered.

The airways were filled with the sounds of Lea gasping for air. Sadness and sounds of crying slowly filled the stillness of the radio station.

Hearing a car approach, then footsteps, Lea moaned weakly and softly begged in broken pleas to the stranger. Tim halted his agony long enough and called out to the person over Lea's car speakers. He was frantic.

"Hello? This is Timothy Serry. Please call 911. Please help my wife." He paused to listen. "Hello?"

"Please, sir," Lea begged the stranger again. "My baby. Oh please help me."

The stranger did not say anything. He only watched this pregnant, dying woman with a sick fascination. In horror and disbelief, the city listened as Lea struggled for breath, begging the stranger to help save her life and the life of her unborn child. Silence blanketed the booth as Lea took her last breath over the airways.

The stranger walked away.

Write, share, and discuss with others your thoughts about this story. Who do you think the stranger was? Did Lea know him? How do you think this story should have ended? Explain why you feel this way.

My Brother's Wife

Ryan

Miraculously gaining admittance to the University of Southern California, I asked my friend Joanna, who interned in student housing, to reach out to her contact in admissions to help ensure that my roommate was at the top of her academic game. Not being the best student myself, it was essential that I graduated from college. Joanna came through with the perfect candidate but discovered that she was already assigned a roommate. It became my personal mission to locate this student and once again begged Joanna for help.

"Ryan, I can get fired for disclosing this personal information," Joanna said, while passing me a copy of the student's ID. "Do me a favor and don't ask me for any more favors."

I gave her a big hug of thanks.

"I won't. You are the best."

With a copy of her school ID photo in hand, I set out to find Shasta Phillips. Not hard to miss, Shasta was a tall, brown-eyed beauty with a bit of an overbite. Pretending to bump into her while dropping my books, Shasta immediately stopped to assist me.

"Thanks for helping. It is tough enough being lost and a freshman. It's even worse when you look clumsy too."

"I kind of look at it as an adventure", she smiled.

"What is your name?", Ryan asked.

"My name is Shasta Philips."

She wore braces and smelled of citrus. Her oversized, floppy hat promised to cover some of the most spectacular hair, judging from the dangling wisps. She was very thin, and wore a locket around her neck. When she spoke, her breath held no scent, yet I found myself sniffing for one. I was immediately intrigued and wanted to know more. I did not know why.

Becoming fast friends with ease, I convinced Shasta that we would be the perfect roommates and she agreed. We hurried to Student Housing and begged the housing coordinator to allow us to room together. Understanding how difficult it is being a freshman and the importance of making friends, the coordinator allowed us to register as roommates.

We were lucky enough to be assigned the old dorm room of the previous RA. Located on the first floor, we were thrilled to not have to climb stairs. The room also had its own private bath, to our surprise. *Another perk of an RA*, I thought. Shasta and I moved into Dorm 3B and started our college lives together as roommates.

Over the months, I discovered that Shasta was the only child of an independently wealthy father who traveled and had recently divorced her alcoholic mother. Desperate to escape the sadness of a mother who was the victim of a long standing affair of her husband and had now recently begun to date, Shasta needed the change of scenery that college offered.

"I will be so happy to have these braces removed from my teeth," she said, while squinting at herself in the mirror. "By this time next year, I will have had my breast surgery and am going to have breasts triple the size of this hilarious A-cup that I'm sporting. Do you think that I would look better with bigger tits?" Shasta immediately pulled up her shirt to expose small breasts that were mostly nipple.

"Girl, you have the chest of a teenage boy. Please pull your shirt down. Look at it this way at least you don't have to invest in bras."

Shooting me the middle finger, Shasta had gotten increasingly comfortable around me and often, like most roommates, walked around with little more on than a panty and bra. Trying not to notice the tingling between my legs at the sight of her playfully caressing her small breasts, I snidely remarked that the surgeon would have to graft skin from her ass just to cover the implants.

We both laughed as Shasta hurried off into our personal shower. *Our shower…what a perfect set up.*

"Hey Ryan, would you mind bringing me the shampoo?" I moved into the bathroom and quietly watched as the water showered over her silhouette of long hair and little curved ass and found myself wondering how it would feel to be inside the shower with her.

"Are you bringing it?"

Hoping that she did not see me watching her, I walked completely into the bathroom, stuck my hand behind the curtain, and passed it to her. "Here it is."

Watching her silhouette up close helped me to gather my nerve to test her response to a quick shower together. Jumping around as if I was about to play sports or get into the ring to fight, I was pumped enough to ask.

"Hey Shasta. What do you think about us—?"

Interrupted by the ringing of the phone, I huffed as I ran to retrieve it. "Hello? Hi, Mrs. Philips." Just as I was telling Mrs. Phillips that Shasta was in the shower, she walked out with a towel around her hair and one around her torso. Until that moment, I never really noticed how stunning she was.

"It's your Mom."

"Hey, Mom." Shasta began to dry her hair then lotion down without even noticing me. *She has so much hair*, I thought. I watched Shasta bend over to shake her hair free, my body began to do its own thing and respond to her movements. I was uncomfortably aroused from watching and needed to release sexual tension. I left the room to shower myself.

Peeling off my clothes, I waited for the water to reheat and stole a moment to appreciate my curvaceous body and openly said, "Any man would want to get with this." I paused. "What about a woman?"

Allowing my hands to move between my legs, I quietly moaned as Shasta's laughs played in the background. With rapid movements, I allowed a sigh of momentary satisfaction to pass through my lips.

"Hey in therrre." Shasta jokingly sang. "Next time, save some for me."

Next time, I will.

After a hefty load of classes and exams, Thanksgiving break was a welcomed one, and having Shasta at my home for the holiday was an extra special treat. Shasta declined a holiday of skiing in Aspen with her Mom and new boyfriend to spend a wonderful time with me, my parents, and brother.

"You know Ry, I just don't think that I am ready to see Mom with another man. My Dad is the only man that I have ever known to hold my Mom's hand, to make her laugh, and to make love to her."

Shasta began to reminisce, as a little girl, of the times she spied on her parents in the hot tub and how watching her Dad kiss her Mom made her feel happy.

"Mom and Dad used to be so in love and so happy until Dad's business trips began to extend into the weekends. His and Mom's favorite song was *Unforgettable* by Nat King Cole and they danced to it often. After Dad left, Mom listened to that song, nonstop. Even though he cheated and left us, Mom was still in love with Dad and wanted him back."

She sighed deeply. "Divorce is like death. Leaving Mom was the most difficult thing that I have ever done, but I was losing myself inside of her unhappiness. I did not know how to console her broken heart when mine was broken also. Mom used me to fill a void that I no longer wanted to fill or feel. I still experience guilt for my selfishness."

As her silent tears turned into a soft weep, I allowed my friend to feel the sadness that I now know she had never allowed herself to feel for fear of not recovering from her own broken heart. Like her Mom, Shasta's Dad was her first and only love also. She too, was mourning his absence. I moved to console her. My friend collapsed inside of me and sobbed for what seemed like hours. She sobbed for the loss of her old life and of her parents' new life. She sobbed for the way things were and the way they will never be again.

I also cried for her broken heart, my powerlessness to repair it, and my desire to be inside of it. She felt abandoned. I placed my hand onto her chin and lifted her head.

"No matter what, I will never abandon you and will always have a shoulder to cry on. You are my friend and I love you." From every inch of my being, I meant those words and would carry them for the rest of my life.

When I arrived at my parent's home, Mom was waiting and ran out to greet us. She acknowledged

Shasta first with a hug. "Welcome to our home, Shasta. We are so happy to have you here. I have spoken to you over the phone so many times that I feel like I've known you forever. You're so tall and pretty too." Stroking her hair, my Mom asked Shasta of her heritage and told her that she looked like Tracey Edmonds with curly hair.

After being greeted by both my Mom and Stepfather, I excused myself to show Shasta to the guest room.

"Ryan," Mom called. "Change of plans. You and Shasta will sleep in your old room, as your stepbrother and his fiancée will be here soon and have decided to stay over. I don't think that she wants to be on the road late at night being 8 ½ months pregnant. I can't say that I blame her."

My heart immediately began to race at the thought of sleeping in the same bed with Shasta. "Sure, Mom. No problem."

After meeting Shasta, my step-brother, was in awe of her, but only spoke of it to me.

"Damn, I would love to tap that ass," he said. "Ry, she is fine. How many men does she have rolling through? If I had known that your girl was bad like that, I would have taken you up on your offer to visit a long time ago."

Reese Abernathy was the apple of my parents' eyes. Unfortunately for me, he had set the precedent of excellence and it sucked. Earning a grotesquely high salary, Reese was on the high road to everywhere. His downfall, however, was the soon-to-be mother of my parent's first grandchild.

Francesca Peltier met my brother at a company sponsored event in Jamaica. She was a server with big *treasures* and an accent that caught my brother's eyes and sperm in the same night. Being a virgin prior to conception, Reese had to admit that the baby was his.

At my parent's urge to do the honorable thing and much more of a guarantee that they will be an active force in the baby's life, Reese convinced Francesca to move stateside with the promise for her to one day become his blushing bride.

"What cha in her' doing?" Francesca entered unexpectedly. "Com'ere girl. Ya hardly sey two words to me."

Hugging me, I noticed the knowing glance that Francesca gave Reese. Women always know when something amiss. As if the big pregnant belly was not enough, Francesca sat unusually close to Reese during dinner, as to re-establish her position for Shasta, who never even noticed Reese. She was, however, extremely inquisitive of Francesca's journey from conception to her current state, and unlike Reese, was always there to serve and insist that Francesca rest. Escorting Francesca to her bedroom for the evening, Shasta quizzed Francesca about her life and pregnancy.

I became engaged in a conversation between Reese and my parents. Reese spoke of Francesca's insistence to be wed prior to their son's birth. If not, his son will not be given the Abernathy last name and she would have her baby and return to Jamaica which would make it difficult for Reese to sue for shared custody. Being Jamaican and poor did not make her stupid. After much discussion and objections, my parents convinced Reese to marry Francesca prior to my nephew's birth to save his rights and for the sake of his soon-to-be son's best interest. I tapped my distraught brother on the arm.

"Next time, be careful where you stick your dick,

stupid. You don't even love her or really even want her, and she is slowly roasting your ass."

After my Stepfather and Reese retired to the front porch to discuss the pre-nup strategy, I asked Mom about Dad. My father and my estranged relationship had widened over the years. When I was twelve years old, my Father relocated to the West Indies and left me, Mom, and my brother Jake alone. It has been almost ten years since I've seen my father. My anger prevented me from visiting him and knew of his existence through the monthly checks that paid child support and now my college tuition. When Jake visited last year, he said that Dad was well and his law practice was thriving. Both Mom and Dad have remarried and appear to be very happy with the way their lives turned out without each other.

"Excuse me, Mrs. Abernathy," Shasta interrupted. "I just want to thank you for a great dinner and for having me here on such a special holiday. You will never know how much it means to spend this time not only with all of you, but with my best girlfriend." The word *girlfriend* was the only word that I heard. Gazing up at Shasta on the stairway, I could not fathom going through life not seeing that beautiful face every day. She was my breath of fresh air.

Feeling someone's eyes on me, I slowly turned to find Reese watching me watch her intently. With a nod and a rise of his glass, I realized, while blushing, that I wore my heart on my sleeve.

"Well," Mom said. "It, too, has been a pleasure having you in our home, Shasta. You should change into something more comfortable and join me for a cup of hot cinnamon cider. It is a Thanksgiving tradition in the Abernathy household."

Waiting for Shasta and Francesca to return downstairs, I approached my Stepfather and gave him a big hug and kiss. Reese Worthington Abernathy II, a devout Catholic by faith and an accountant by trade, was one of the most intelligent men that I had ever met. He stepped in to raise us when my Mother was at her weakest and simply needed someone to rely on.

"I miss you and am so thankful that Mom has you. I just wanted you to know that. And I miss being home this time of year to help put up the Christmas decorations."

The decorating of the Christmas tree was another holiday tradition in our household. Every year my Stepfather selects the biggest tree from the tree farm and Mom buys a new ornament for each of us to commemorate the holiday year. This year, she included an ornament for Francesca, Shasta and the soon-to-be Reese Worthington Abernathy IV.

"Cider's here," Mom said, placing the tray on the table. "Reese do you need help locating the Christmas decorations?"

"Got them," he responded.

As my stepfather gave his yearly speech of Thanksgiving blessings, I could hardly contain the joy I felt for having such a supportive and loving family. I felt sadness for Francesca, whose family was so far away, and Shasta whose parents were not available. After the decorating of the tree, everyone said their goodnights and retired for the evening.

With my shower was taken, I walked around enjoying the familiarity of my old bedroom, then slowly climbed into bed with an already sleeping Shasta. One too many spiked ciders had taken her into a deep slumber of soft snores and whirrs. Watching her lying on her back, legs slightly bent, and a partial breast exposed, I recalled the conversation in the car about her father and suddenly wanted to kiss her lips in hopes to fill that chasm of pain that was slowly consuming her. I positioned my face to slowly draw in the scent of her hair, her skin, and her breath. I just wanted to be near her, but felt guilty and dirty for the thoughts that I had about my unsuspecting friend. I found her attractive, but did not consider myself a lesbian because I still wanted men.

I remember the very day that I realized that I liked girls.

My cousin, Lotion, was wilding out over her new-found lesbian sexuality and wanted to share it with the world. She had been experiencing this Asian chick named June, who turned her out in a major way. A self assured woman, June had been in the game for a long time and could smell a newbie from many miles away.

When my cousin, Lotion, decided that she wanted to sample, June was more than happy to become her buffet. Unfortunately, Lotion never suspected that June had no boundaries was ready and willing to take over her next victim, me. I was introduced to June at the nightclub Sensual. Her lingering soft embrace made me feel uneasily excited. She had the dominance of a man with the softness of a woman. She was masculinity with breasts. Her deep smoky voice was hypnotizing. Her hair was cut close to her face, which displayed exquisite cheek bones. Her tight jeans lightly shielded her slim, muscular tone. She was beautiful.

Lotion danced with others and felt confident in my babysitting of June, coming by occasionally to sneak a kiss, get a feel, and sip her drink. When June slipped me her number, I felt excitement knowing that this woman found me attractive but wanted to escape her presence. She was intimidating and made me feel uncomfortable in my own skin, so I went to the restroom.

Taking deep breaths in a stall, to calm my discomfort, June quietly called my name. I froze and held my breath as I did not want to take this any further.

"Ryan," June called. "I know you're in there. I can smell your innocence." I said nothing. "I want it Ryan". This woman had lost her mind coming into the bathroom to sex me. "I want to feel your lips as they swell against my tongue in anticipation of exploding. I want to take your tits and rub them on my cheeks while gripping that tight virgin ass of yours with my hands."

She cannot be serious.

"I want to take my strap, bend you over, and work you until you lose your fucking mind."

Coming out of another stall, a patron who knew June engaged her. "Damn, June. If that bitch doesn't give it up from that, we can take this party back to my house and work it out." She began dancing to her own words and left singing, "Work it out, work it out!"

"Ryan!" *Thank God.* Lotion had tire of dancing and noticed that neither June nor I was sitting where she left us.

"I'm in here," I answered.

"What's up? Can't piss by yourself?" She laughed, but waited for an answer. "What's up baby?" Her attention diverted to June. "Got a little something for Momma? *She* needs some stroking."

I heard the stall door slam then deep moans of pleasure that paralyzed me and prevented my feet from moving. I wanted to feel the heat of lesbian lovemaking and did not think that spying in the next stall was such a bad thing.

"I'm leaving," I said and knocked on the walls. "I'll see you outside."

I walked to the door but the sounds of their passion pulled me back into the bathroom. I closed the door pretending to leave. I listened to zippers zipping down and hard slams against the wall. My body sweltered as Lotion went to her knees while pulling June's jeans down. The sound of sucking and ass slapping forced me to put my fingers between my legs. I stifled my heavy breathing to mask the pleasure that I was giving myself. I was on fire and needed an extinguisher.

The bathroom door flung opened and the drunk lady who challenged June earlier, returned for another pee. I silenced her as she walked into the bathroom and encouraged her to listen as Lotion and June became totally immersed and lost to the world. The drunk lady started to kiss my newly exposed breast. I allowed her as it was not her face that I was seeing, it was June's. This beautiful drunk lady put her soft, round breast towards my mouth, which I eagerly opened to receive. It was salty and sweaty. Just like that, I wanted more.

I sucked harder and eagerly as she whimpered. I covered her mouth with one hand and ripped down her panties and fondled her with the other. Her *sugar* was so wet that my fingers drowned inside of them. Quietly and quickly, her body jerked uncontrollably and it was over. When she began to move her mouth downward on me, both Lotion and June began to squeal with release from the buildup of sexual dancing from the dance floor to the bathroom. I quickly pushed the drunk lady away and ran out the door before being spotted. I was embarrassed but was left wanting more.

Sweaty and flushed, the cool air outside felt refreshing and was a welcomed visitor against my skin. I wanted to be out of that place and home. I wanted to be cleansed of that dirty woman who sucked my breast and kissed my neck. I wanted to wash away the pleasure that I gave her as my entire hand disappeared inside of her, finding her G-spot and making her body shake like an earthquake. This was not my life and I wanted to rid myself of anything that reminded me of it.

Contemplating leaving, I saw the drunk woman emerge from inside the club. She was obviously looking around for me and now looked quite sober. I turned to walk away and bumped into June who had been watching me.

"What's up?" She asked.

"Nothing. Just getting some fresh air 'cuz that place is hot. Where is Lotion? What's up with you two, anyway?"

Shifting, June took a deep breath as if she was going to give me this long speech as to why it was not really working, but instead said only that she simply did not want to hurt her.

"Call me," she said, pulling out her cell phone. "I want to taste you. Give me your number. I'll look you up in a few weeks."

As I tell her my number, Lotion emerged. "What's going on?"

"I'm just staying in contact with June."

"What for? You trying to fuck her or something?"

June said nothing. She just walked away and left me to .fend for myself.

"No," I lied. "June said that she was looking for a job and I was telling her to give me a call next week because I know of someone in her line of business. You need to lighten up."

Not really able to tell if she believed me or not, she motioned for me to get in the car while she spoke with June. All seemed well on the drive home, but I never forgot what happened in the bathroom that night. I never did call June. Since that night, I had not explored another woman and had never really experienced a man in the way that it should have been enjoyable. I was standing at a crossroad in my young life and was willing to willing to re-visit the unfamiliar- familiar but was afraid of the truth that came with it.

I lay there in the darkness admiring Shasta's silhouette from the moons hue. I could not recall ever having feelings of wanting to be with anyone so deeply. It felt so innocent and intimate. Different. For all the sleepovers that I held and attended, I would have thought that something would have surfaced, but nothing. It has been said that we mirror the people that are most like us. Maybe Shasta felt this way also. Like me, she was too afraid to say anything. *How would I know?* I had heard numerous stories in college where girls stepped out of their boxes and became lesbians overnight. Maybe I was falling into that statistic. *Would I be embarrassed? Would I care?*

I shook her lightly, "Shasta, are you awake?"

She groggily opened her eyes. "Yes, I am now. What is it?"

In the darkness, I became brave. "Have you ever been kissed by a woman?"

Wondering why she was asked that question, Shasta hesitated to respond. She, indeed, had never been kissed by anyone, much less a woman. She had always been what now seemed incredibly overprotected to the point of dependency on her Dad for any mental or physical affection she needed. Her Dad had always told her to save herself for her husband and to remember that any physical contact, even something as small as a hug, leaves a part of you with that person. Therefore, if you did not want that person to own a part of you, abstain.

Shasta had always done that, except for with her parents or close family members.

"I have not ever been kissed by anyone other than my Dad. I am saving myself for my husband or at least someone who is deserving of my affections. I am not ashamed of it. I have never entertained the idea of a woman kissing me in an intimate way. Nor will I ever."

Her voice was both defensive and offended. I quickly grabbed her hand.

"It's nothing to be ashamed of and I wish that I had that kind of willpower. I am proud of you for holding true to the values that your Father instilled."

Feeling the tension in her hand relax, I thanked her for being the beautiful person that she is and for being my best friend. Although she never spoke another word about that evening, I could feel the core of our friendship shift. I just did not know if it was for the better or worse. Choosing to ignore the air that had gotten heavy with quiet curiosity, I turned and fell asleep.

Friday morning brought a frenzy of first-day holiday shopping. Mom, Shasta, Francesca, and I were out the house at the break of dawn to fight the masses. Taking a break and enjoying Starbucks, I noticed someone approach Shasta at the pickup counter. I watched her smile and toss her hair and could not help but feel a little jealous. Shasta had seemingly come a long way in a short period of time. She was turning into a confident butterfly.

Distracted by the loud laughter behind me, I turned to see Mom squeezing the breath out my brother, Jake. He had called earlier to say that he was in town for the day and wanted to see everyone. My big brother was gorgeous and intelligent. Basking in Jake's light, Mom took the opportunity to tell everyone that passed her by that her son graduated at the top of his class and passed the bar. *Great, another lawyer and more pressure.* When she finally let him up for air, Jake threw me the peace sign and I ran into his arms.

"What's up, Ry? I hear you been partying it up at school and not focusing on your studies like you are supposed to. What's up with that?"

Jake could not tolerate what he thought was waste and at this moment, he envisioned my wasting Dad's hard earned money and thought that I needed a lecture. Just as I was about to defend my partying, Shasta caught Jake's eyes and I was immediately off the hook. After the introduction, both Shasta and Jake conspicuously moved away from the masses to find a quiet spot in the midst of chaos.

"Ooh, Ry, they will make some pretty and smart grandbabies for me," Mom said dreamily.

"Don't forget, rich", I added. "Shasta has a boatload of money, housekeepers, gardeners, driver and all that shit at her disposal." Mom raised an eyebrow, which meant, *"Watch your mouth."*

I told Mom that Shasta's parents were divorced and really rich but she was emotionally alone. Mom began to tear.

"That poor girl, she said. "She must be sad and lonely without the closeness of her family."

Never really thinking about it that way, I imagined that Shasta was indeed probably very sad inside and lonely. But looking at her smile and laugh with Jake, loneliness seemed to be the farthest thing from her mind.

Before moving to chapter two, write down your thoughts about this story thus far. What do you think happens next? What emotions surface as you read this short? Explain why you feel this way.

Shasta

Returning from a long morning of shopping, Shasta wanted to feel the wind on her face and told the family that she needed to go for a run. Shasta started at a slow trot down the beautiful scenic highway then burst into a full run. With the quiet sounds of thunder surrounding her, she allowed the misty rain to wash her as she slowly began to process the coincidence of running into Jake after all of these years. How could I have ever guessed that he was a member of Ryan's family? *She thought.*

Jake and I met five years ago at a pool party. With the both of us being too boring to appreciate a real party and being non-drinkers at the time, we escaped inside to eat chips and talk. As teenagers, Jake and I became fast friends. We talked often but never about Ryan only that he had a sister, both his parents had remarried and that he lived between the two. Early on, we decided, as teenagers sometimes do, that we loved each other and would one day marry. He was supposed to be my first kiss…my first everything. Without notice, my parents sent me to boarding school. We eventually lost contact with one another but I never stopped thinking of him.

I should have said something, I thought. But it was such a sudden surprise when Jake approached me and even more so, when I realized that he and Ryan were family. Jake and I agreed that we would keep our history a secret. *But why, I wondered, we were innocent friends.* I was younger when I met Jake but he still had the ability to make me feel special and I wanted to feel that again. Deciding that not disclosing was the right thing to do for now, I turned to make my way back. I was happy to be going home tomorrow and relax with Ryan.

Content to be back in our own space, Ryan and I relaxed with a bottle of wine and soft jazz. We both had begun to doze from the soft high when *Unforgettable,* started to play. I began to sob from the heartache of knowing that my parents would never dance in love again. Ryan immediately awakened and held me close. Hearing this song for the first time without my Mom present was more than I could handle and triggered an unexpected flood of emotional heartache.

"It's okay, Shasta. I am here for you. Cry as much as you need. I got you," Ryan reassured. Noticing, but not really absorbing the softness of Ryan's body, I felt the nakedness on parts of her exposed stomach and thighs. Her arms held me gently and the softness of her skin was comforting. I wanted to be closer and held tighter, but was too ashamed to ask. Ryan stared intently into my tearing eyes and began to rub her cheeks lightly against my face. Her hands slowly caressed my back. I moved into her, wanting to feel more.

Afraid but willing, I closed my eyes to what was happening but kept my senses open. Ryan slowly uncoiled my hair and it fell unto my shoulders. Her lips softly caressed mine then became more persuasive. I opened my mouth to taste more of her full lips. Laying me down, Ryan intimately moved her hands over my small breasts then with her tongue. I allowed a moan to escape my lips and was thankful for the darkness, which hid my facial enjoyment. With never a word spoken, Ryan worked on my body like a mechanic working on an expensive car. She was careful and meticulous. Kissing my stomach and thighs, I could not believe the sensations that were moving throughout my body. I could have never imagined that my highest level of intimacy, for the first time, would be with a woman. For a brief moment, I thought of Jake.

After much anticipation, Ryan spread my legs and slowly began to manipulate her tongue in various ways, making love to me. Unhurriedly at first, she tasted the outside of me and I no longer cared who heard my passion calls. When she began to thrash feverishly on my *honeycomb* and slide her fingers inside of me, I could only succumb to the trembling that overtook my body.

My body now still, Ryan moved my hands between her thighs. Hearing her moan my name, I suddenly became ashamed, pulled my hands back and pushed her away. Afraid that she would become angry with me, I ran into the bathroom, first sitting in a panicked silence then fervently washing myself---to scrub away the humiliation for enjoying the touch of a woman. I scrubbed so hard, that my skin began to welt. I felt dirty and humiliated and wondered if I was a lesbian. When I finally emerged from the bathroom, Ryan was gone.

Wishing that I could journey through Ryan's mind, but could not, I decided to journey through my own asking myself questions. *What the hell happened between us? Was this something that Ryan had planned all along? For all the times that I walked around half naked, what was she thinking? Was she in love with me?* I had every intention of asking Ryan these questions upon her return, whenever that would be. I just needed to know.

I attended class the next day, but was not focused. I intentionally sat in the back of the class to see if Ryan would show. She did not. I was worried, but not worried enough to call her Mom to see if she was there. She returned home later that evening, as if nothing had happened between us.

"Hey, Shasta. S'up? Did you miss me while I was gone? That Christmas concert was banging!" Coming in like a whirlwind, Ryan was full of enthusiasm and glee. I had completely forgotten that Ryan had made plans, during our Thanksgiving visit, to go to the concert with her Mom. So consumed by my own reasoning, I assumed that Ryan was dealing with her own emotions from the experience that we shared. I felt stupid.

"What's going on?"

Not really waiting for an answer, Ryan busily began to unpack her bags, sorting the dirty laundry from the clean and putting them away. She shared how much fun she had with her Mom and other family members in Atlanta. Listening, I imagined her out of those jeans and standing in nakedness. I found myself wanting to move closer to smell her skin and press my body against hers. I missed her and felt guilty for wanting her in the midst of all of my emotional confusion.

Ryan mentioned that she did not realize that Georgia had so many great places, like Sambuca's in Buckhead that served up the live jazz as well as a great steak. She talked about the boutiques and the nightlife as it was the first time that she had experienced the city.

"I bought a gift for you, Shasta." I wondered why did she not talk about what happened the night she left.

"Are you alright?"

"Yeah, I'm cool."

"You like it?" It was a beautiful brown lambskin jacket.

"For sure! That is beautiful!"

"Cool. Then you need to get on the horn and thank my Mom," Ryan said laughing. "Because you know a sister be broke and can't buy snap."

Dialing up Ryan's Mom, I watched Ryan as she undressed and walked into the bathroom, pretending not to observe her as she moved through the close quarters. As much as I wanted to, I could not ask her how she felt about that night. I did not want to be *that* girl, so I just let it go.

Ryan began to spend less and less time in the dorm and more time with what she affectionately dubbed as her flavors. This particular flavor, Greg, was lasting a lot longer than most and was keeping my roommate away from home often. I missed her and longed for her presence, laughter, and secretly, her kisses. I had mentioned to Ryan earlier that I was planning to go home and visit my Mom during spring break. Unfortunately, Mom had other plans. While en route to the airport, Mom called to say that she would not be home until the weekend and wondered if I'd mind either staying home until she returned or wait to fly in the weekend.

I was not a priority on her list any longer and graciously said that I would see her in a couple months and to stay in touch if she planned to travel abroad. She promised to email her itinerary for the next month so that I would always know where and how to contact her. *She has an itinerary now, sigh.* Feeling rejected and sorry for myself, I stopped into an airport bar to decide where I would now vacation for my spring break.

"You look as if you just lost your best friend," said the man on the next stool. "Can I buy a drink for you?" Fat, bald, with broken and openly spaced teeth, he was the sad epitome of the traveling salesman. He also had a severe perspiration problem. Disgusted, I simply turned and stylishly strutted away in my five-hundred-dollar Jimmy Choo's.

At the last minute, I decided to go home anyway and take a break away from school and the thoughts of loneliness. How I longed for the days when both my parents would welcome me home with open arms of love after being away. I was the center of my parents' world then and the only thing that they lived for was to make me happy. Now they lived to make themselves happy and not really care what happened to me, it seemed. I phoned ahead and told Maria, the housekeeper, to take the next few days off with pay. I simply wanted to spend some time alone to sulk. She told me that she'd put fresh linen on my bed and have dinner waiting in the oven when I arrived home. I thanked her and wished her a pleasant long weekend.

Walking through the door immediately brought back all of the familiar scents of home. The fresh baked cinnamon rolls and the authentic Mexican dinners that Maria always cooked for me. When I think back, there are not many events in my life where Maria was not present. She was there with me the first day of school, my first period, my first boy crush, all of my birthdays, and graduation. She was the one constant in my life that I have always depended on, but never thought I needed.

"Hola, Shasta."

Startled, I turned around. "Maria! I thought that you were gone!"

"I would never allow you to come home to an empty house."

"You look beautiful, Maria."

I was happy to see her. She always thought of me first and knew just what I needed even when I did not.

We talked for a while, waved our goodbyes and I watched Maria drive away. Exhausted, I put on some Boney James, filled my bathtub with bubbles, poured a glass of wine and relaxed. It was nice to be at home without interruption.

I had everything that I could possibly want in life and my life was still a mess. I was not only alone, I was lonely. I drank some more and closed my eyes while I begged my mind to temporarily stop moving. Hearing the phone rang, I dragged myself out my semi-drunken state and answered the phone.

"Phillips' residence."

"What's up?" An energetic voice comes over the phone. "What the hell you doing at your Mom's crib and not answering your cell? Can't tell a sista when you jetting?"

"Hey Ry, what's up? I just decided to chill at home since Mom stood me up. You were hanging with your flavors, so I decided to literally jet home." Not even pretending to sound energetic or even excited that she interrupted my pity party, I told her that I just wanted to be alone.

Taking a more concerned tone, Ryan asked if I needed her there. I lied and said no, but really could have used some time with someone who cared about me, man or woman. Ryan was on her way to her Mom's and said she would call once arrived. We hung up and I decided to have one more glass of wine. I awakened to someone asking me if I knew my name. With my vision slowly focusing, I found myself looking into the face a stranger with kind brown eyes, asking if I was alright. To my left there was a police officer and to my right, there was Ryan.

She looked worried and had been crying. Trying to sit up but feeling dazed, I asked, "Who's hurt?" Everyone began to laugh at me.

"You are, fool."

"What are you talking about?"

Showing a sigh of relief, Ryan explained. "I felt that you were not yourself after our last convo, so I called Mom and told her that I was going to check on you instead of heading home today. When I got here, you would not come to the door or answer the phone, so I called the police. They broke in and found you on the floor with your naked ass sprawled out and blood around your head. We thought someone had broken in until we saw the empty wine bottles and realized that your drunken ass probably tripped getting out of the tub and knocked yourself out! Thank God you are alive."

"So, how many people saw my coochie?" I whispered. Ryan laughed and pointed out the two officers who arrived on the scene to find me lying on the bathroom floor. "Well, at least they are fine." I said, slightly embarrassed but still tickled.

I refused treatment and Ryan opted to stay home with me, promising to keep a watchful eye to ensure that I did not suffer any concussion like symptoms. After the medical team and locksmith left, Ryan called my Mom and updated her on my condition.

"She is resting, Ms. Philips. I will have her to phone you in the morning." Sighing, "She's not cutting her trip short to come check on me personally, is she? No need to respond, I already know the answer. Goodnight Ryan."

In attempts to lift my spirits, Ryan moved closer and pulled the covers from my body, exposing my nakedness. "I'm going to tell you a bedtime story.

Shasta. That bedtime story will include tasting, touching, hugging and licking. You wanna hear it?"

"No."

"Sure you do."

After ensuring that I felt every lick, touch and hug, I fell into a deep slumber and still without tasting Ryan.

Ryan and Greg became closer and decided to move in together, leaving me to live alone. She continued to visit but our connection had shift. She never attempted to make love to me again. With Ryan, I experienced love. She was my best friend and my confidant. I missed her and I missed her touch.

Ryan became pregnant her last year of college and married Greg before the birth of their child. I was a bridesmaid in her wedding and became the Godmother to her son, Ellington. Life moved along and Jake and I re-connected, with Ryan's approval. Ryan and now Jake remained uninformed of each other's past roles in my life. A few years later, I married Jake and became the mother of two children of my own. Ryan's and my physical love affair ended but our psychological affair continued on. The guilt of loving a brother and sister was stressful but worth it. She was worth it. I still connected with Ryan in a way that I would never connect with Jake.

One year later, Jake opened his own law firm and invited Ryan and Greg to spend the weekend with us to celebrate. The excitement of seeing my first lover was almost too much to contain. I imagined all the things that we would do and was anxious to hold Ryan's body close to mine once again. Ryan finally arrived and was stunning. She wore both motherhood and marriage well.

Stopping short of running into her arms, I greeted Greg first so that I could hold my first love closer, longer.

After dinner and drinks, Ryan and I spent the evening sitting and talking at home, while the guys went out for billiards. Happy to be in our own space, I pulled Ryan close to me and slowly kissed her face, neck, and hands.

"I love you so much, Ryan."

We both began to breathe heavily. Ryan kissed my lips softly then pulled away.

"Shasta, we can't do this anymore. You are my brother's wife."

"But it's okay, Ry. It's not like we have kept our affair going. I have never forgotten those nights and have always regretted being afraid to taste you. I am more confident and less selfish now and just want a chance to finish what we started. Please, just let me take you upstairs and make love to you. I have waited years for this opportunity."

"Shasta, if we began again, it wouldn't stop with tonight. We are connected mentally but cannot re-connect physically. I have lived my life trying *not* to love you anymore. When I gave you my blessings to date and marry Jake, I let you go as a lover and embraced you as my *brother's wife.* I also knew with this, I could never touch you again.

"I thought you did that to keep me in your life, not keep me out of it."

"It's over, Shasta."

Without another word, Ryan walked upstairs and left me sitting. I began to cry and could not believe that it was really over. Knowing that she was right did not make the hurt any less. My heart was broken because I wanted her more than I wanted her brother. Jake appeared to find me crying.

"What's wrong Shasta? Why are you crying? Where's Ry?"

Through my tears, I told Jake of my college affair with Ryan. She was breaking my heart which made it that much easier to share. Jake could not process what he was hearing.

"I wanted to protect you, Jake. That is why I have never told you." Jake began to pace.

"Ryan was a great friend when I did not have anyone, Jake. She had no idea back then that you and I knew each other. We agreed not to share that information, remember, so I never told her. We were teenagers in love not lovers. I should have told her. We would have not become lovers, if I'd told her. It was coincidental that you were family."

Through clenched teeth, Jake asked, "So all along, throughout our dating, our children, and now, you have been having sex with my sister?"

"No. It stopped before we graduated."

"When was the first time?"

"Our first time happened after the first Thanksgiving with your family."

"So, you could have stopped it, then?"

"It wasn't that simple, Jake. I already had an emotional attachment to her. I just didn't know that it was a sexual one as well. It just happened but I loved it and loved her."

He asked in disgust, "So you are in love with her?" I dropped my head so that I would not have to witness Jake's hurt and fury.

"Are you in love with her, Shasta?!"

For all the times that I wanted to scream to the world that I loved this woman, when I finally had my chance, I could not.

I wanted to calm the confusion that was forcing me to reckon with what I had just done to this family. I was once the lover to both a brother and sister. One was in love with me and I was in love with the other. My selfish heart said that it could have worked if Ryan had not left me. We were one, Ryan and I. *Doesn't she know that, I thought?* We weaved into each other like a maze. Ryan's touch, after all these years, still melted me as if it was the first time. Her kiss burned my skin and left me longing for more.

She was soft and understanding where he was firm and uncompromising. Yet, they made love to me with the same exactness. Hers felt better. To me, they were one. Their bodies owned the same softness, and smelled of the same natural scent. I wanted them both. The warmth of new tears trickles down my face. I was relieved and prepared myself for the inevitable divorce from the man who placed me on a pedestal of perfection. I was the mother of his children, but his sister was in the delivery room. I said I do to him at the altar but his sister owned my heart.

Jake angrily began to move towards the stairs to confront Ryan. Calling for Greg, I moved to stop Jake, grabbing his shirt but losing the grip when he jerked away.

"Ryan!" He yelled, as he took the steps by two's. "Ryan, you lesbian bitch, where are you?" Thanking God that all our children were at his Mother's, I yelled for Jake to stop. He did not. Jake reached the top of the stairs, ran down the hallway, and kicked in the bedroom door.

To his surprise, Ryan was not in bed. Checking her bathroom and the other bedrooms, Jake's anger intensified each time he failed to locate her. Feeling that she was still inside of the house, I began to look around. Her purse and coat were still on the sofa.

"Jake, let's just go to a hotel so that we both can calm down and talk about this tomorrow."

"No! I am going to kill that lesbian bitch when I get my hands on her. How dare she sleep in my house and fuck my wife!"

"She's not fucking me, Jake! And if she is a lesbian bitch, what am I? Do you want to kill me too?" Jake slowed his pace.

"No, you are my wife, Shasta, and you did not know any better. She took advantage of you."

"She did not take advantage of me! We were lovers and loved one another. I was with her willingly. She filled a void in my life then that you still cannot fill now-even in her absence. She is my best and most trusted confidant and I—"

Before I could complete my sentence, strong hands grabbed my neck and began to squeeze. I slowly felt my feet leave the floor and passed in and out of consciousness, all the while looking into the face of my deranged husband. A gunshot fired and Jake's grip slowly released.

Falling to the floor, I caught a glimpse of Ryan pointing the gun at him with tears flowing down her face. He was shot in the shoulder. As she stood in the silk pajamas that I bought for her last week, I notice just how beautiful she was standing there.

Jake recovered and lunged toward Ryan. She was caught off guard and fired randomly. As I fell back onto the floor, I saw my life with my husband, my lover, and my children flash before me and then felt the pain. Ryan dropped the gun and ran towards me with wild eyes of horror and catches me before I fall to the floor. I saw her mouth move but there were no sounds. Jake is on the phone but I cannot hear his words. I see Greg appear. He moves the gun away. I am afraid. Ryan inhaled my last exhale.

Ryan's Song

Looking back at the photos, it should have been obvious to everyone that we shared more than a just a friendship. The connection was so clear that it still astounds me. I sometimes weep when I think of Shasta. I killed her. My Dad returned to assist in the preparation of my defense while I remain in jail.

Write, share, and discuss with others your thoughts about this story. Would this have happened if Jake and Shasta shared their history? What emotions surfaced as you read this short story? Explain why you feel this way.

Black Angel

Seems like I am carrying the weight of the world on my shoulders and nobody cares about its heaviness but me. I am still young in years but being tired seems to already be my way of life. My existencc, at best, seems mediocre, but the day's events will soon prove me wrong.

Daylight came this morning with the cussing of Black Angel. She's my Momma. GranNan said that when Momma was born, she was as black as the midnight sun—which actually ain't black at all, but I ain't telling her that—with the face of an angel. She said that Angel's Momma's sins were burnt into Angel's soul, which was the soul of a woman who died drinking, fussing, and cussing while pushing Black Angel out into a life of easy lays and hard lessons.

Most people don't know that I know things. GranNan says it's a gift but it scares me sometimes. 'Cuz when you're eight years old, you just don't understand why you hear things that ain't nobody else hearing and see things ain't nobody else seeing, sometimes before it even happens. Black Angel says she dunwanna hear no shit about nobody sittin' beside her in a room that she can't see. So, when I see um', I jes don't say nothin'.

Before my brother Colby was born, I saw my Momma pregnant. When I told her what I wanted her to name my brother, she said, "Chile, you crazy. Ain't no mo' babies comin' out of here."

Seven months later, Colby Angel Alexander was born. He white and I ain't. Our daddy is white with sun-tanned skin and big ole blue eyes.

They hold lots of secrets, I can tell. He said that when he met Angel, her essence was as hot cayenne peppers and he just had to get a taste of those spices. I'm a result of the first taste. Colby was the next.

We been living with GranNan since Momma got hooked on the street life of clubs, drinking, drugs, and sometimes, prostitution. She look tired and old for her twenty-six years and coughs a lot. Sometimes I watch her weep in quiet and hold a picture of herself, like she remembering who she used to be and don't like what she is now.

She sings sad songs about lost love and broken hearts. It's weird 'cuz when she's on the streets, she talk a whole lotta mess or "talkin' shit," as GranNan would say. My gift always tryna show me a dark around Angel but I hurry up and blank that away 'cuz it sits deep in my lil soul and makes my stomach hurt.

Today, we gettin' all dressed up 'cuz my Daddy's goin' to church with us. GranNan says it's time to introduce Colby to the Lord and be baptized. She has been up bakin', shellin' peas, and snappin' green beans. It smells so good.

"Good mornin', GranNan," I said, giving her a big squeeze and kiss. "Can I help you fix Colby's special dinner?"

Smiling, GranNan pushed the bowl of peas over for me to help shell. "GranNan, when I got baptized, I remember seeing the Lord. He was pretty." She never took her eyes off me while listening.

"Jesabella, you got tha' gift and the Lord got special plans for your old spirit. Keep your eyes open chile.

Keep your eyes wide open." She moved the bowl away. "Now stop eatin' those raw peas and go get your wash off. Then come back for breakfast."

After washing off, I went into the room that I share with Black Angel to get dressed. Momma is still beautiful sometimes. She likes to lay across the bed in naked. She is staring right through me while smoking a cigarette, which she knows GranNan don't like. Feeling uncomfortable, I turn my back to get dressed so that she can't see my little acorns. I reckon they will be as big as Angel's someday, jiggling all over her chest. But I won't put lotion and glitter all over mine so people can see 'em, like she does.

"Girl, what you trying to hide?" Black Angel laughed. "You got a long way to go before any man will look at you. But when they do, you better be ready 'cuz you are already a stunner. Don't look nothing like me but look just like me. What kinda shit is that?"

Knocking on the door but not waiting, Melody walks in.

"Hey girl, what's up?"

Melody Letinna is Angel's friend. I call her Mel. GranNan don't like her 'cuz she said they do nasty stuff to each other like always hugging, kissing, and laying around together. Sometimes when GranNan is at church, Angel turns on the TV for me and Colby in the living room while she and Mel go into her room. Then she pulls the curtains across the door and makes funny humming sounds. Angel told me that if I peek, my eyes will burn out, so I never peek. But I know it's the same sounds that she and Daddy used to make when she was still a good Momma and not this Momma.

"Hey, Jizzy," Mel said.

Angel had given me that nickname because my hair was red and frizzy. Since folks be on this new thing about combinin' names and mine is Jesabella and my hair is frizzy, I am called Jizzy. I don't hate it so much 'cuz I don't hate me so much. I think I am kinda pretty, but in a different way. My brown skin, green eyes, and frizzy red hair, leaves me never mistaken or forgotten.

I don't look nothin' like Daddy, but Colby is his spitting image. GranNan says I am a cross between Daddy's momma who has red hair with green eyes and my grandmother, Esther, whose skin was the color of caramel candy. GranNan says one day Imma be the talk of every man's lips but I shouldn't listen.

"Jizzy, are you excited about Colby's baptism?" Mel asked.

Hurrying to pull my dress up, "Yes." And walk out of the room.

I sat down at the dining room table and waited for Daddy and Colby. I wore GranNan's robe over my dress to make sure that I didn't spill anything on it.

"Knock, knock. We're coming in."

"Daddy!" I screamed and sprinted to the door to give him the biggest hug ever.

"Look at my little beauty queen."

Blushing, I hugged him tighter, wanting to never let go.

"Wizzy." Still learning to pronounce the letter *J*, Colby punched my arm and ran past me to GranNan.

"GwanNan!" Colby ran into GranNan's arms of love, warmth, and safety.

Slowly emerging from the bedroom with Mel following closely, Angel coldly greeted Daddy.

"You look tired, Angel," he said. "Sin City is getting the best of you, huh?"

Whispering cuss words under her breath, Angel stuck her middle finger up to Daddy.

"Hey, Baby CoCo," Angel said, as she reached her hands out to hold him.

"No." Colby buried his face into GranNan's chest. "GwanNan hold Colby not Angel."

Turning fiercely towards Daddy, Angel approaches him where her face is almost touching his.

"You tryna turn my kid against me, whitey? He ain't no white boy. He my son! You thank just cause the courts say you can have him mean he all yours. He's mine too! I'm his damn Momma! I gave birth to him!"

With tears streaming down her angry face and arms flailing, Colby begins to cry and yell "Go way, Angel! Bad Angel." Angel, never losing eye contact with Daddy, speaks to Colby.

"I am your Mother, son. You have my spirit and my energy. When I am dead, my moving spirit will protect you when yo' white ass daddy can't." Mel softly pulls Angel into her. "I'm a good momma, Mel," she exclaimed. "I'm a good momma. I'm a good momma". Feeling like I am seeing way too much, I grab Daddy's hand. *You ain't,* I thought.

"Chile, go and get yourself together and meet us at the church in thirty minutes," GranNan ordered. "We going on down to the church to get this baby ready. Jesabella, grab that bag with Colby's change of clothes. James, get that box with the food and let's go. Y'all done ruined this baby's day before it even gets started. But God's got this one and He asking to save his lil' soul and we gon' answer."

Black Angel never made it to the baptism. When we got back, all her stuff was gone and I no longer felt her spirit within my body. We never heard from her again. When GranNan got sick and went to heaven, I went to live with my Daddy. At GranNan's funeral, Angel sat beside me but ain't nobody seen her but me.

Write, share, and discuss with others your thoughts about this story. Did Jizzy really have the gift? What emotions surface as you read this short story? Explain why you feel this way.

*** COMING SOON ***

The Blue Pages

Shim

The softness of the voice. The smoothness of skin. All these things clearly contradicted what was penetrating me. My mind refused to allow my eyes to open as the voice begged for me to see its owner. I was afraid. The owner knew this. The laugh was feminine but the strokes were of a male owner. My body betrayed me and responded. Why was I enjoying this. I opened my eyes. The same dream four nights in a row.

The Last Truth

I get so excited watching him sleep. As the years pass, he becomes more and more beautiful to me. Sexy. His skin is as smooth as a Boney James' tune. I wonder what he thinks when his eyes are closed. He is a great provider, a great father, a smooth and attentive lover. Life is good. I look at that bold wedding band that defines his left hand. It speaks stronger than any words. He carries that commitment like a preacher carries a Bible, faithfully and with pride. I am his wife. He is my husband. It just keeps getting better. So, how do I introduce him to the death that is certain to take my life and probably his?

Foot Warmer

Sometimes it snows in April and when it does, the poor gets a lil bit colder while da' other half gwoin' off to some place hot. Us women gotta keep dem' massers hot, while doin what dey wives won't do. But we don't mind sometimes 'cuz we having Massers' babies wit' clear skin and curly hair. A house nigga to be da' foot warmer fer dey chilren while keepin warm deyselfs. When no one's looking, we sneaka drank outta Massa's milk jar and swalla hard to get da las fill. We don't usually get real cow milk, jes what the slave mammas squeeze out for dey babies. But sometimes, after I push out Masser's babies, he warm up to me an grab one of de' titties that his babies be suckling on an den tells me that my tits belongs to him and him alone.

Made in the USA
Columbia, SC
27 April 2022

59548982R00096